"I don't want you to go to Florida."

"Why not?" She stood in front of him, arms crossed.

"Because we're arguing and stressing. Stay here—work on our relationship."

"Okay, then don't go to Costa Rica." Seemed simple enough to her.

"I already put down money."

"Ah, I see. You can do what you want, but I can't."

"No, Julie. Don't put words in my mouth. I'm just saying I've already paid money."

She stared into his brown eyes for a long moment. Her bottom lip quivered, but she had a clear mind when she said, "We need a break, Ethan."

He sighed, running his hand through his dark waves. "You're right. Let's take a night together this week." He stepped toward her and gripped her hand with his hands.

"No, we need a break from each other." The words sank like heavy boulders into her heart.

He squeezed her fingers. "What do you mean?"

Clarity braced her. She knew what she had to do. "Ethan, since we've been married, all we planned for was our future children and buying an old farmhouse off Craven Hill Road. Now that we don't have that plan anymore, all we do is pick and fight with each other."

"So running off to Florida is going to solve that?"

"No, I'm not talking about just Florida. I'm going to ask Bobby and Elle if I can stay with them until I go."

RACHEL HAUCK lives in Florida with her husband, Tony, a youth pastor. A graduate of Ohio State University, she worked for seventeen years in the software industry before leaving to write and work in ministry. She is also a speaker and worship leader. Rachel served the writing community as president of American Christian Fiction Writers. Visit her Web site at www.rachelhauck.com

Books by Rachel Hauck

HEARTSONG PRESENTS

HP574—Lambert's Pride with Lynn A. Coleman

Lambert's Code

Rachel Hauck

Heartsong Presents

This story was written while enduring two hurricanes, Frances and Jeanne. I'm grateful to my remarkable husband for doing most of the cleanup after Jeanne so I could write. He's my best friend, encourager, editor, and "babe." What would I do without him? *Lambert's Code* is dedicated to Tony.

Special thanks to Louise Gouge for her critique and to my editor and friend, Susan Downs.

A note from the Author:
I love to hear from my readers! You may correspond with me by writing:

Rachel Hauck
Author Relations
PO Box 719
Uhrichsville, OH 44683

ISBN 1-59310-704-8

LAMBERT'S CODE

one

Ethan breathed in the rich aroma of coffee wafting from the kitchen as he jogged downstairs and dropped his gym bag in the hall by the front door.

"The league basketball championship is at five, Julie. You coming?" He kissed his wife on the cheek and broke off a piece of her muffin.

"No, my doctor's appointment is at four. Are you coming?" Julie raised a brow as she handed Ethan a cup of coffee. "Muffins are in the box." She sat down at the breakfast nook.

Taking the coffee, he paused. Her words echoed in his mind, *"Doctor's appointment." Am I supposed to be at this appointment?*

Pondering her question, he pulled a plate from the cupboard and picked a blueberry muffin from the box marked PERI'S PERK.

"I see Peri's coffee shop is making its mark here in White Birch, New Hampshire."

"She brought our cozy community into the twenty-first century." Julie sipped her coffee.

Ethan leaned against the counter, biting into his breakfast. He wished he'd whipped up a batch of eggs instead. He set his plate aside. "Am I supposed to go with you today?"

She picked at her muffin. "Only if you want to, Ethan."

He regarded her for a moment, thinking how tired she sounded. They were both weary of this medical process.

"Do you think you can handle this one by yourself? I have a lot of work to do today, and I need to be at the rec center by four thirty."

She regarded him with wide green eyes. Most of the time, they sparkled when she looked at him, but not this morning.

"Well, of course, the rec center is more important."

5

"Come on, Jules, you know that's not true."

"Do I?"

He sighed. "Julie, I've been to Dr. Patterson's OB-GYN office more than most of the women in this town."

She tipped her coffee cup and drank slowly. After a moment, she said, "Not lately. Besides, I thought we were in this together."

"We are. Why would you even say that? But today, can I have a pass?" He stooped to see her face. "Please, Mrs. Lambert, may I have a get-out-of-the-doctor's-appointment pass?" He flashed a cheesy grin and raised his left eyebrow.

She gazed into her coffee. "What if it's bad news?"

"It's not going to be bad news." He kissed her forehead. "Everything's going to be all right, babe. Don't spend the day worrying." He pulled her to her feet and wrapped her in his arms.

She dropped her face to his chest and held him like she didn't want to let go. "I won't."

But he knew she would. With a quick squeeze, he released her, his thoughts already on the day ahead.

Ducking into the pantry, he shoved food boxes around, hunting for pregame energy. "Do we have any protein bars?"

"Not unless you bought them."

"Babe, can we organize this pantry? Throw some of this out or give it away? I don't think we'll eat half this stuff."

"Have at it."

Ethan peered around the door. "Are you okay?" He tossed a couple of breakfast bars on the counter.

I wonder if Mark Benton will make tonight's game. He counted on big Mark for rebounds. If Mark couldn't play, he'd have to spend some of the afternoon finding a replacement center. White Birch didn't grow men over six-foot-five every day.

"I'm fine," Julie said, staring out the nook window. "But you can clean the pantry as well as I can. In fact, you're better—"

The phone's ring interrupted her rebuttal.

Ethan made eye contact with Julie as he answered. "Hello?"

She gave him a quick glance and slight smile.

"What?" he said after a moment. "I'll be right there." He slapped the phone onto the wall cradle with a disgusted sigh.

"What's wrong?" Julie moved behind Ethan with her plate, setting it in the kitchen sink.

"The environmental inspectors are on their way to Lambert's Furniture again." He pointed to the plate in the sink. "You want to put that in the dishwasher?"

She stuck out her tongue. "Neat freak."

"Slob."

Julie tucked her plate away in the dishwasher and flipped off the kitchen light. "I need to get to school."

He captured her for a kiss, her oval face serious and beautiful, like the cello music she loved to play. "I need to get going, too. Are you sure you're okay?"

She smoothed her hand over his chest. "Nervous, I guess."

He handed Julie her navy peacoat from the front closet.

"Babe, it's going to be fine. Don't assume the worst."

"It's been three years, Ethan."

He hesitated. "I know." He slipped on his trench coat. Three years and thousands of dollars. They'd be in a house now, instead of the apartment, if only—

He shook the thought loose. No sense in rehashing the past, second-guessing their decisions. *What's done is done.*

Outside in the cold, clear morning, he fought a twinge of guilt, watching Julie walk to her car. *Should I go to the doctor's appointment?*

But what about the game? He felt sure he'd reminded Julie a month ago about the championship. The first game started at five. If they won, they'd play through the winner's bracket. He had every intention of winning the championship trophy.

If he met Julie at the doc's office, he'd never make it to the rec center in time to warm up.

If he gives us bad news, I'll miss the game altogether. He banished the thought from his mind. *It won't be bad news. It won't.*

Unlocking his Honda, Ethan tossed his gym bag into the

backseat and glanced over the car's top as Julie pulled out of the apartment parking lot. She waved and tooted her horn good-bye.

Maybe I should call her. He reached for his cell and was about to dial her number when his phone rang.

He answered, "Ethan Lambert."

"Ethan, it's Mark Benton. I won't be able to make it to tonight's game."

&

"Listen up, it's time to think about our spring concert." Julie passed out sheet music to the White Birch Elementary fifth-grade orchestra students. "Take these home. Practice them."

A collective groan filled the room. "It's only February, Mrs. Lambert."

"I know, I know. But let's start practicing now so you don't sound like a pack of hungry alley cats on a rainy night."

The girls giggled, the boys snickered, and when Cole Gunter started caterwauling, the whole class joined him.

"All right, all right." Julie held up her hands for silence, laughing. "If that noise doesn't frighten you into practicing, I don't know what will. Make sure you don't sound like that for the spring concert. And, Cole, let's get you signed up for chorus."

The ten- and eleven-year-olds laughed. Julie ruffled Cole's hair.

When the end-of-class bell rang, the kids scurried for the door, banging their instruments against the doorway on their way out. Julie cringed at the sound of the cases crashing against metal but called after them, "Don't forget, practice!"

She glanced at her watch. Three thirty. A nervous twitch made her feel lightheaded. In thirty minutes, she'd be in Dr. Patterson's office. The pizza plate she'd picked for lunch didn't seem like such a good idea right now. She pressed her hand on her abdomen. *Please, Lord, please let him have good news.*

Julie stared out the classroom window for a few minutes, waiting for a trickle of peace, fragments of the past few years flying through her thoughts. She'd been so hopeful when they sat in Dr. Patterson's office three years ago. He'd regaled them with success stories, explained the newest procedures and medications.

So far, none had worked for her.

"You still here, girl?" Sophia Caraballo strolled into Julie's classroom, hands on her hips.

Julie turned from the window. "Yeah, just thinking. I should grade these papers, though." She walked to her desk, motioning at the pile.

Sophia picked up the top sheet. " 'Why I Love Music.' "

"Come on, Sophia." Julie reached for the paper, but Sophia slapped her hand away. "I love music because it makes my mom smile after my dad yells at her." The svelte, overdone blond peered at Julie. "Now, *that* is sad."

Julie snatched the composition from her friend. "Yes, it is." She filed the stack of papers in her shoulder tote. "Now I've got to go or I'll be late."

"You nervous?"

"No." She regarded Sophia. "Yes. Well, more anxious than nervous. I'm trying to let go and let God have control of the situation, but it's hard." Julie walked to the door and flipped off the classroom light, picking up her coat from the wall hook.

"What do you think he'll say?" Sophia walked with Julie down the hall toward the front doors.

"That everything is all right. Give it more time." Julie gave Sophia a halfhearted smile. She ignored the fretful emotions that challenged her confidence.

"Is Ethan meeting you there?" Sophia asked.

Julie shook her head. "He's busy today."

"Busy? Are you kidding me?" Sophia grabbed her friend by the arm. "What a cad."

"He's not a cad, Sophia. He does have a lot on his plate, running production for Lambert's Furniture."

"So much he can't make this important appointment? His cousin is his boss, for crying out loud."

Julie sighed, not wanting to hash out her marriage issues

with the school secretary. Despite her friendship, Sophia had a gossip's tongue.

"I'll talk to you later." Julie gave her a small hug and shoved open the glass door, cold air rushing past.

Sophia shivered. "Call me, okay?"

"Okay."

On the trip across town to Dr. Patterson's office, Julie's anxiety increased. She tried to pray with faith, but after the years of trying, failing, and trying again, her hope waned. "Lord, give me courage, please."

It bothered her that Ethan didn't want to come. She was as weary of the medical process as he was. Even more so. How could he leave her alone for this important appointment, the one that could make or break their hopes? He'd missed one or two before, but this one. . .

In the waiting room, Julie fidgeted in her chair and wondered why she'd bothered to press the speed limit to be on time. "Hurry up and wait," she muttered to herself.

She flipped through a parenting magazine before realizing what she was doing. She tossed it aside. Fishing her cell from her purse, Julie dialed Ethan. If she reminded him, he might come. Maybe. But he didn't answer his cell or office phone.

"Julie, you can go back now." The nurse behind the glass smiled and motioned to the inner-office door.

"Thanks, Amy."

"Good to see you."

"You, too."

In Dr. Patterson's wide, cluttered office, Julie lowered herself into the soft leather chair across from his desk.

"Well, young lady, how are you today?" Dr. Patterson came in after her, chipper and smiling. He sat with a thud in his worn leather chair.

Julie clasped her hands in her lap and leaned toward him, as if to draw on his gentle strength. "Fine, thank you."

He smiled. The lines of his weathered, kind face fanned out under his eyes, and his demeanor calmed her inner turmoil.

"Everything going okay?"

"You tell me," Julie said with a light laugh but winced thinking how glib she sounded.

Dr. Patterson chuckled. "Guess I am the doctor." He opened the file in front of him and reviewed information.

Julie shifted, straightening her skirt and adjusting her wedding ring. Corkboards, cluttered with pictures of Dr. Patterson holding naked newborns in his hands, lined the office walls.

Her heart palpitated at the idea of a child, her child, Ethan's child.

Dr. Patterson closed the folder. "Is Ethan joining us today?" He looked directly into her eyes, his expression molded with compassion.

Her eyes burned as she shook her head no.

"Should we call him?" Dr. Patterson placed his hand on the phone. "I can move a few things around in order to wait for him."

Julie swallowed the lump in her throat. "He's working, then he has a basketball game. I'll give him the news."

"A basketball game?" A flicker of concern flashed in Dr. Patterson's eyes.

"It's the league championship." Julie managed a smile. "You know how Ethan loves sports."

"Well, if you're sure, I'll go over the results with you. But if you and Ethan need to come in together, just give Amy a call. She'll get you right in. What you and Ethan have been through can put a strain on a marriage."

"Yes, I know. I appreciate your offer." Julie wrapped her arms around her waist and cuddled against the back of the chair. For a split second, she didn't think she could endure waiting for the news.

"I ran every test in the book, Julie. I even consulted with Dr. Llewellyn down in Manchester. He has a great deal of experience with infertility matters."

"Second opinions are always nice." She tried to sound confident.

The doctor slowly rose and walked around his desk, sitting in the chair next to her.

The chair that Ethan should be sitting in.

"You're scaring me." She trembled, and her tears spilled.

He took her hands in his. "I know how much you and Ethan want children."

Julie freed her hand to wipe her cheeks. Dr. Patterson leaned over his desk for the tissue box.

Taking the one he offered her, Julie blew her nose and balled the tissue in her hand. "This is not going to be good, is it?"

"Well, it depends on your definition of good."

She smiled despite her tears. "Grandchildren for my parents."

Dr. Patterson sighed. A chill slithered down Julie's spine.

"My dear, unless God intervenes, the test results show that you and Ethan have a very, very slim chance of conceiving and an even slimmer chance of carrying a child to term."

"No, please, Dr. Patterson." Julie shook her head, sobbing. "There must be something else we can do."

"We've done all we can do, Julie."

"But I've gotten pregnant before. Surely—"

"Yes, nine years ago, and you miscarried."

The words pierced Julie's heart as if the news of her miscarriage were fresh and current. She'd convinced herself it was the business of college, grad school, and Ethan's long days learning the production of Lambert's Furniture that prevented them from conceiving again.

"The endometriosis caused a lot of scarring." Dr. Patterson spoke with care. "Your womb can't support a pregnancy."

"What about a second surgery? Can't surgery correct it?"

Dr. Patterson shook his head and comforted Julie with a fatherly touch on her shoulder. "The last surgery didn't improve your situation. With a second, you risk more scarring. Perhaps God has other plans for you and Ethan."

Julie's shoulders slumped, and she buried her face in her hands. Dr. Patterson slipped his arm around her. She leaned against him and wept.

two

Late in the afternoon, Ethan pressed SEND, e-mailing the last compliancy report to the environmental inspector's office. He felt spent, his day consumed by the tedious review of Lambert's Furniture's environmental practices.

He'd not planned to answer waste disposal questions for the second time in six months. His to-do list looked the same this afternoon as it did this morning. And he still needed a big man for tonight's game.

"Is the inspector's report done?" Will Adams, Ethan's cousin and president of Lambert's Furniture, came in and sat down.

Ethan nodded. "It's done, but, Will, those guys have to leave us alone. That's the second visit."

"I know, but we want to cooperate. Otherwise, they'll think we're hiding something."

Ethan leaned back, hands clasped behind his head. "Guess this is why you pay me the big bucks. I didn't get an industrial engineering degree for nothing."

Will laughed. "Big bucks? If that's what you want to call it, you're more than welcome. I wish I could pay you big bucks."

Ethan chuckled, shifting to work on his computer. "Well, when we get this new warehouse built, then we'll talk. I didn't have time to call the contractor, by the way."

Will checked his handheld personal data assistant. "Let's meet on that tomorrow morning. The new warehouse is key to our growth."

Ethan clicked on his computer calendar. "What time?"

"Nine is fine."

Ethan glanced at Will. "Bet Grandpa never imagined his little wood and whittle company would ever get this big."

Will tapped on his data assistant, nodding with a smile. In

13

another second, he looked up and said, "Ethan, I drove past Milo Park on my way back from the town council meeting."

"Yeah?" Ethan typed in his reminder about tomorrow morning's meeting. *Meet with Will re: warehouse contractor.*

"Julie was there, sitting alone on one of the benches."

Ethan glanced at his watch for the first time all afternoon. Four thirty. Already? *Wow, I need to get to the rec center and start warming up.*

"It's snowing. She was sitting in the snow."

Ethan clicked icons on his computer, shutting it down for the day. "I'll ask her about it tonight."

Will stood. "Do. Something didn't feel right. I wish I'd stopped to check on her."

Packing up his laptop, Ethan glanced up just as Will exited his office. He was about to comment on his introspective wife when a brilliant thought flashed across his mind. *Will can play center. He's tall, athletic. He played some basketball in school.*

He dashed around his desk and bound down the hall. "Will, buddy. What are you doing tonight?"

❧

Julie felt one with the snow, cold and frozen. Falling flakes powdered her head and shoulders while Dr. Patterson's words fluttered across the plains of her heart.

Unless God intervenes…a very, very slim chance of conceiving. In her whole life, she had never felt as hopeless as she did now. Not even when she miscarried the first year of their marriage.

"You're young. You'll have more children." Everyone said so, even Dr. Patterson.

But today his diagnosis bore an entirely different message. *I'm barren.* Julie thought. *At twenty-eight, I'm barren.*

Tears slipped down her chilled cheeks. She wiped them away with her gloved fingers, squelching the scream that pressed against her soul: *God, it's not fair!*

But she restrained the words from riding on the wind. What good would it do to yell out? What change could it bring?

A sharp wind brushed through the park, tugging at her hair

and hat. Three years of trying for a child, and this was the end of their hopes and fears.

At least now she knew.

I should go home. But she didn't move. If ever she needed to pray, it was now. But her words felt shallow and inadequate. "Lord, I don't understand."

From her coat pocket, Julie's cell chirped. She hoped to see Ethan's number on the tiny screen. For the first time since she'd left the medical center, she longed for his comfort. But the caller ID flashed Sophia's name and number.

"Hi, Sophia." Julie tried to sound cheery and light.

"Well, what did the doctor say?"

Her vision blurred. Julie looked over the snow-covered park and pursed her lips, contemplating her answer. The news felt personal and private. She hadn't even told her husband yet. How could she broadcast the news to her friend, the gossip?

"Julie?" Sophia pressed.

"He said—" She hesitated before continuing. "It might be awhile."

"Aw, girl, are you kidding?"

Sophia's tone provoked more tears. Julie pressed her gloved fingers against her eyes. "It's no big deal."

"No big deal? Since I met you five years ago, you've wanted babies."

Julie lifted her face to the falling snow, drawing a deep breath. "It's okay, Sophia."

"What did Ethan say?"

Julie inhaled, the cold air numbing her emotions. "Nothing. I—"

"Nothing? The man said nothing?" Sophia's voice spiked with indignation.

"I haven't told him yet."

"Why not?"

"Listen, I'll talk to you tomorrow."

"Meet me for coffee at Peri's Perk in the morning."

Julie agreed, thinking how Peri Cortland's hip coffee shop

had rejuvenated the town's morning routine. A cup of her freshly brewed coffee would cheer her day.

"See you in the morning."

"See you at Peri's."

Julie pressed END and stood, brushing the snow from her coat. She plowed through white drifts to her car and climbed behind the wheel. When she turned the key, the car responded with a clicking sound.

"Oh, come on. Not now." She clenched her jaw and tried again.

Nothing. The car's engine would not turn over. Julie dropped her head to the steering wheel and pounded the dashboard of her twelve-year-old economy car. "God, this is not fair!"

She'd have a new car if she hadn't convinced Ethan to try for one last round of fertility treatments. He'd wanted to wait another year, rebuild their savings, give their emotions a break, but she'd argued fervently against him.

In the end, what little money they'd set aside for a down payment was spent, and it still wasn't enough. Her parents, eager for grandchildren, loaned them the last of the money they needed. At the time, Julie felt so sure she would conceive. Now, looking back, all she could think was what a waste it had been. All that money spent with nothing to show for it.

When she didn't become pregnant, Dr. Patterson insisted on a thorough battery of tests.

I'm barren. Barren. The word echoed in her soul like the *tick, tick, tick* of a clock in an empty room. *Barren, barren, barren.*

Julie jerked her head up. *I've got to get moving.* She tried the key again, but the old engine refused to fire.

She yanked open the door, grabbed her purse and shoulder tote, and stepped out into a foot of snow.

જ

Sweaty but exhilarated, Ethan drove home from the rec center, the large championship trophy sitting in the seat next to him, the seat belt clicked around his treasure.

Don't want it bouncing all over the car, do I?

He grinned, turning down Main Street, cruising past Milo Park. The hue of the amber-colored streetlight reflected off the new fallen powder, and Ethan, well, he couldn't resist a sudden impulse.

He pulled into the park and bounded toward the winter wonderland. He flopped on his back, pumping his arms and legs to make the perfect snow angel.

With a hooting laugh, he hopped up without destroying his creation and flopped down in the snow for a second snow angel. Then with his bare finger he wrote "Ethan" under one and "Julie" under the other.

How long had it been that way? Ethan and Julie. Forever, it seemed to him. Since they were sixteen.

Chilled from his romp in the snow, Ethan jogged back to his car. Out of the corner of his eye, in the dim light of the streetlamp, he saw a little car buried under mounting snow.

Is that Julie's car? Ethan swerved right to investigate. He brushed the snow from the hood to see the chipped paint of her faded blue heap. *Yep, it's hers. What's it doing parked here?*

Suddenly he remembered. *Will.* What did he say about Julie sitting in the park? He'd forgotten all about calling her.

Returning to his car, he revved the engine and blasted the heater. Digging his cell phone from his sports bag, he autodialed home. Julie did not answer.

Next he called her cell. He let it ring until voice mail picked up. Then he dialed home again. Still no answer.

He drummed his fingers against the steering wheel. *Julie, where are you?* He called her cell one more time. She didn't pick up.

Come on, Jules, where are you? He took a deep breath and exhaled slowly. *She's not at home and apparently not with her cell. Yet her car is abandoned at Milo Park.*

Ethan tried to remember her weekly schedule. What night did she help the church youth choir? Lately their schedules took them in opposite directions. *Thursdays,* he concluded. *She works with them on Thursdays. Today is Monday.*

Ethan tapped his cell phone against his chin. After a few seconds, he dialed a different number. The crisp, aristocratic voice of Ralph Hanover answered. "Good evening, Hanover residence."

"Hi, Ralph. It's Ethan. Is Julie there?"

"No, son, she's not."

"Have you heard from her?" Frustration laced his words.

"Let me check with her mother."

Ethan waited, listening to the muffled tone of his father-in-law. "Sandy hasn't talked to her since Saturday."

"Thanks." Ethan started to press END, but Ralph continued. "Did you two quarrel?"

"No, sir, we didn't. She's just not answering the home phone or her cell."

"I see. Don't forget Friday night. Sandy's planned a big party. She wants to cheer everyone from their midwinter doldrums."

Friday, right. "Yeah, I'll talk to Julie."

Ralph cleared his voice. "She's never missed one of Sandy's parties. Don't see why she should start now."

"It's been a tough week, Ralph."

"All the more reason to join us." His words sounded so final. No was not an option.

"Good night, sir."

"Good night, son."

Ethan tossed his phone into the passenger seat. Ralph and Sandy Hanover never ceased to exert influence on their only child's life. When were they going to be grandparents? Shouldn't Julie try out for the New Hampshire symphony? Julie somehow managed to obtain a healthy amount of independence, but she also carried a certain level of obligation. Deep obligation.

"Wife, where are you?" Ethan squinted in the darkness. Surely she was safe. *Lord, help me out here. She's safe, right?*

three

In the living room, Julie graded papers, her legs crossed Indian style, a carton of Chinese food on the floor beside her.

"Julie." Ethan charged through the front door, his voice like a foghorn.

"Ethan?"

"Why didn't you answer the phone?" He stood in the middle of the room, his coat askew, a trophy under one arm and a basketball under the other.

"I see you won." Julie motioned to the golden guerdon. She picked up the beef and broccoli carton.

"You didn't answer my question." Ethan didn't move.

Julie kept her eyes averted. If she looked at him, she'd burst into tears, and quite frankly, she didn't have the energy to go through it again. She'd tell him the news, but not tonight. Not now. *Where would I find the words?*

"I took a bath." She omitted that she was just about to sink into the sudsy water when he called the first time.

"Why didn't you call me back?"

"I knew you'd be home soon, and I needed to get these papers graded."

"Why is your car at Milo Park?" He walked past her to the spare bedroom they referred to as the den. "It's practically buried in snow."

Julie bit her lower lip and stared at her students' papers, not really seeing the words. She heard Ethan's movements in the study, the bounce of the basketball against the hardwood floor, the shuffle of items on the computer desk to make room for his prize.

"Jules? What happened to your car?" Ethan called from the den. "Gave me a good scare seeing it abandoned there and you

19

not answering the phone. I called your parents to see if you were over there."

She chewed slowly on another bite of beef and broccoli. "I thought you were taking the trophy to work."

"I will." Ethan stood over her. "Why won't you answer my questions?"

Julie set the carton aside, stacked her students' papers on the end table, and strode toward the kitchen. "Do you want some dinner?"

"Yes." Ethan smiled. "The Chinese smells good."

Mechanically Julie retrieved a plate from the cupboard. Ethan hated to eat from the carton. While she served his plate, he filled his glass with ice and water from the refrigerator.

I can't tell him now. I can't. Tomorrow. She felt weary and frayed.

"Who did you play?" She handed him a plate of Wong Lee's finest, plastering a smile on her face. Though proud of her athletic husband's win, her heart could not rejoice.

"Creager Technologies. Beat the pants off of 'em. Will played center for us."

"Good for him."

Ethan sat at the table, laughing. "Ol' Jeff played for Creager." He slapped his knee. "He huffed and puffed up and down the court the whole time."

Ethan's merriment infected her a little. She leaned forward, elbows propped on the kitchen counter, picturing Ethan's police officer cousin, Jeff Simmons—burly like a grizzly bear— playing basketball.

"How'd he get roped into that job?"

Ethan scooped a mouthful of fried rice and teriyaki chicken with his chopsticks. "Ten bucks says Elizabeth got him into it. Since she started at Creager Technologies, she's enlisted several of the cousins into their league teams."

"It's dangerous to be a Lambert cousin in this town."

He gazed at her, serious. "Is it dangerous to be a Lambert wife?"

"What? Of course not."

"Okay, then tell me what happened to your car. Why is it at Milo Park? And by the way, Will said he saw you there this afternoon, sitting in the snow."

Feeling exposed, Julie went to the living room and reclined on the couch. "I went to the park to think. When I went to leave, the car wouldn't start."

"Babe, why didn't you call me?" Ethan twisted toward her.

She lifted her head. "Call you? You were too busy to—" She stopped short.

"Too busy to what?"

"You know what." She struggled to contain her anger. *But I should be angry.*

Ethan ate in silence. After a few moments, he asked in a low tone, "How did you get home?"

"Walked."

"All that way?"

"Yes, the exercise felt good."

He let loose a wry laugh. "You? Exercise? What's wrong?"

"Nothing."

He fell silent, then asked abruptly as if he suddenly remembered, "How was your doctor's appointment?"

"Fine." She stopped before her emotions betrayed her.

"Fine?" He regarded her, waiting for more.

"Just fine." She rested her arm over her closed eyes and breathed deeply.

Ethan walked to the kitchen with his plate. "See, I told you the news wouldn't be bad."

"Right." She swallowed hard.

"So why did you sit in the park under the falling snow?"

"Felt like it." Julie heard the water running from the sink and then the click of the dishwasher.

"But everything's fine?"

No, it's not. It will never be fine. "Sure."

Ethan's touch on her leg startled her. "What exactly did Doc Patterson say?"

"Ethan, my head is killing me. Can we talk about this later?" A thought flashed through her mind that changed Julie's weepiness to resolve. *I want a new car.*

Ethan squeezed her leg. "Sure. I'll call the tow truck in the morning." He disappeared down the hall.

She bolted upright. "Ethan, I want a new car." *Can't have a baby? I'll get a new car.*

His head popped around the corner. "What?"

"I want a new car."

"Babe, we're paying off debt. Medical bills, school bills, your parents."

She stood. With quick movements, she adjusted her baggy sweats. "I'm tired of that ol' jalopy. It's held together with bubble gum and duct tape. You said so yourself."

Ethan chuckled. "No, the mechanic said so."

Hands on her hips, she raised her chin. "Jesse knows what he's talking about."

With a shake of his head, Ethan answered, "I don't want to spend any more money, Julie. Think how great it will be to pay off our debt. And, for the first time in a year, our savings is above zero."

She bristled. "In the meantime, I drive around in a twelve-year-old piece of junk."

"That piece of junk has another good year or two left. Peter-John Roth drives the same make and model, and his car runs like a top. It has to be fifteen, sixteen years old."

"I want a new car, Ethan." She couldn't put her emotions into words, but suddenly the idea of driving a new car captivated her.

He sighed and drew her to him, kissing her softly. "Don't cry, Jules. Maybe we can look in the fall when the dealers have sales. It's not just spending money for a down payment; it's adding the monthly car payment I don't want right now."

She stiffened, tugging on the sleeves of her sweatshirt. "It's my money, too. I work, bring in an income."

"Right, and that's what goes to the debt."

They argued for several minutes over who could make the call on spending money for a new car. Julie thought since she worked, she should be able to use her money the way she wanted.

"Does that theory apply to my salary, too?" Ethan asked.

They went around until Ethan stopped the conversation.

"I don't understand your sudden urgency, but can we talk about this later? I need to go over some things for work tomorrow."

"Sure."

When he left for the den, Julie tiptoed upstairs to the bathroom, kicked the cabinet, then wept.

❧

Ethan stared at the open document on his laptop screen but didn't read it. The championship trophy stood guard over him. He clicked the page closed, the desire to work abated.

Falling back against the desk chair, he propped his hands on his legs. *What happened here tonight?* He came home, admittedly a little angry. He asked about her car, asked about the doctor's appointment. She said everything was fine. She listened to his championship game recap. Then suddenly the squabble over a new car ignited.

Something wasn't right, but he didn't know what. He wanted to press Julie for an explanation, but lately, if he pushed her, she went deeper within herself.

When did their communication become so hard? Since eleventh grade, she'd been his best friend. They talked about everything.

Ethan wandered out to the living room, his body stiff from the night of play. He collapsed in his chair and clicked on the television. Blankly he stared at the images on the screen.

The last few years had been difficult. As they waded through the waters of new careers, stress wove its way into their lives, even more so once they realized starting a family would not be easy. Dr. Patterson was hopeful in the beginning. Julie took a year off work while she completed grad school, hoping to conceive.

Then came the special treatments, medications, and one surgery. Their small savings depleted, her parents loaned them money. A gift, they said. But Ethan insisted on paying it back.

Meanwhile, Ethan worked his way up in the family business, starting on the production floor at the same pay rate as all the others on the crew. Those were lean years.

But by now, Ethan wanted to be more financially solvent. At the very least, buy a house. He'd never factored in the cost of conceiving a dream.

What sparked the idea in Julie to buy a car? She'd been more than happy with her old vehicle until tonight. She'd rather spend money on medical treatments. Last year, they'd had a whopper of an argument over money and the value of their unsuccessful fertility treatments. But tonight, she had a different look in her eyes.

He checked the mantel clock. Eleven thirty. He'd been home for over two hours, and as on most nights, he sat up in the living room while she read upstairs and fell asleep with the light on. They were in the same place but definitely apart.

The urge hit him to run up to his wife, his best friend, and wrap her in his arms, promising that everything would be all right. He'd done that after their first newlywed arguments, though lately. . . He wondered when resisting became so simple.

Ethan pointed the remote control at the plasma screen and upped the volume. He felt exhausted from the emotional turmoil. Trying to have a baby was one thing, difficult and disappointing. But losing touch with his wife burdened him. He slumped down in his lounge chair, closed his eyes, and listened to the noise.

≥

Julie drew the down comforter up to her chin, the resonance of television laughter bouncing up the stairs. Emotionally drained, she tried to pray, knowing she needed the Lord's comfort. But her thoughts twisted around Ethan and how she wanted him to come to bed. She ached to snuggle next to him and bury her face in his chest. Her heart longed to hear him promise everything would be all right.

When did they stop talking face-to-face? Were they the same two people who sat up all night in her family's basement game room, talking? The two who bought cell phones with anytime minutes the moment they could afford them?

She should confess Dr. Patterson's conclusions. Yet if he wanted to know, if he cared, he would have made it to the medical center. Fifteen minutes. All he needed to surrender was fifteen minutes. Her disappointment over his lack of interest only made her barrenness more pronounced.

"Lord," Julie cried out in the darkness, "I can't go on like this."

Burrowing under the covers, she sobbed until her soul released its burden.

Sleep eluded her, and the longer Ethan stayed downstairs in front of the TV, the more her sorrow turned to anger.

She went to the bathroom to blow her nose. *All he cares about is sports and winning a basketball trophy.* She crawled back into bed with a burning in her middle.

"Lord, do something with him." She rolled over on her side, determined to think of something else—like a new car.

I need a new car. My old broken-down heap is on its last leg. She felt sure her parents would prefer she drove a reliable car over paying back their loan.

When Ethan tiptoed upstairs and slid into bed, Julie remained awake, her back to him.

The bed gave way to his long, lean frame as he adjusted the sheets and blankets to suit him. She wondered if he would reach for her, as so many times in the past when things weren't right between them.

When they first married, they agreed never to go to bed angry or discontent. Many a quarrel had been resolved on this very bed. Remembering caused familiar feelings to stir in her heart. When did they first bend the rule? Had they broken it completely?

To Julie, life itself felt broken.

Ethan, if you reach for me, I'll respond. Despite her anger, she yearned for his touch. She craved his kisses on her hair, her face, and her lips. She wanted to lose herself in his safe embrace.

Making up her mind, Julie inched toward the center of the bed and lightly touched her husband's back with her fingertips. He did not stir. The soft sound of his breathing filled the air around them.

Julie moved back to her side of the bed. *How can you fall asleep so fast, Ethan?*

She tried to sleep but couldn't. Images of her future loomed before her, blank and void, without the melody of children's laughter, without porcelain faces molded with her eyes and his nose.

Long into the night, Julie finally fell into a fitful sleep.

four

In a sleepy stupor, Ethan slapped the alarm button and rolled out of bed. He showered and dressed, then checked his data assistant for the day's action items while slipping his keys and wallet into his pockets. He clipped on his cell phone and tied on his shoes.

"Julie," he called. He caught her made-up side of the bed in his peripheral vision. If he didn't know better, he'd wonder if she'd slept next to him at all.

But he remembered how warm the bed felt when he climbed in a little after midnight. He'd wanted to reach for her but didn't, considering her mood when she went to bed. Besides, she seemed to sleep so peacefully.

"Babe, I thought we'd grab a little breakfast on our way in this morning. I can drop you off at school afterwards." Ethan leaned out the bedroom door, fastening on his watch, his ear tuned to the sounds of the house. Silence. He sniffed. No coffee.

"Jules?" Ethan ambled downstairs. "Julie?" *Did she leave already?* Her carton of beef and broccoli from last night remained on the living room floor. But her school papers were gone.

With a shake of his head, Ethan tossed the leftovers in the garbage. Back in the den, he found a note from Julie tacked to his new trophy.

Ethan, Sophia came by for me. We'd planned to have coffee at Peri's anyway. Julie

Ethan crumpled the note, juxtaposed between ire and relief. He wished she'd told him she was leaving, but hopefully today would be better than yesterday.

He sat down in his desk chair. "Lord, we're in a rough patch, aren't we? Give us grace. Give *me* grace."

A thought flashed through his mind. What about a nice romantic dinner at Italian Hills? *Hmm? Good idea, Lord.*

Candlelight? Soft music? Julie would love it. She could forget about her cares in the peaceful ambiance and enjoy fine cuisine. Ethan made a mental note to secure a reservation for six o'clock.

Snapping up his cell, he dialed the familiar number of his grandpa and grandma Lambert.

"Hello?" The soothing voice of the Lambert patriarch eased down the line.

"Grandpa, it's Ethan." He cradled the phone on his shoulder as he packed up his laptop.

"How's my favorite grandson?"

"Is it my week to be your favorite?"

Grandpa chuckled. "It is if you're inviting me to breakfast."

"How'd you know?"

"Why else would you be calling me so early?"

"All right, if you know so much, what's Sam's special today?" He hooked his laptop bag on his shoulder and reached for the trophy.

"All-you-can-eat pancakes with a side of bacon and eggs."

"Guess I'm buying then." With a chuckle, Ethan grabbed his coat from the closet.

"I'm the retired old guy. Of course you're buying."

"Deal," Ethan said, locking the front door behind him. "See you at the diner."

Hopping into his Honda sedan, Ethan shifted into gear and backed out of his parking slot, pausing to look through his cell phone contact list. If Julie liked driving a stick shift, he would trade cars with her. But she'd contended she liked her automatic, albeit dilapidated, car.

He pressed TALK when the screen flashed MEL BROTHERS' TOWING.

❧

"If you ask me, he's an insensitive clod," Sophia said with

conviction before sipping from her grandé caramel coffee topped with whipped cream.

Julie tore at her napkin. "He didn't know."

As disappointed as she was in Ethan, Julie defended her husband. She blamed herself for Sophia's skewed perception. She'd painted a bad picture of him lately, and she resolved to change that image.

"You should have told him then." Sophia waved her long, manicured finger in the air.

Julie swirled her latte. "I couldn't form the words. Then, all of a sudden, I wanted a new car, so we argued over that."

"Girl, you need a new car."

"I know, but—" She stared out the coffee shop window and wished she was sitting with Ethan instead of her acerbic friend.

"If you ask me, he'd rather play sports than raise a child anyway."

"Sophia, stop. That's not true."

"Seems to me he's always finding some jock thing to do."

Julie pressed her fingers to her temples. "Can we please change the subject?"

"To what? My dateless life? There are no good men, I tell you, none."

Oh, but there are good men. Ethan. "You're just not looking in the right places."

"Where shall I look? Church?" Sophia rolled her eyes and shifted in her seat.

Julie jabbed her in the arm. "Don't knock it until you try it."

Sophia immediately changed the topic and launched into the latest politics of White Birch Elementary School and the status of the new building budget. "By this time next year, we should have a dozen new classrooms."

Julie sipped her coffee. "Do you think I'll get that new music room?"

"It's in the plan." Sophia winked with a nod.

"Wouldn't that be amazing?"

"Yes, but don't hold your breath. Until they hand you the classroom key, anything is possible."

Julie sighed. "So true."

"Speaking of teaching—" Sophia pointed to her watch. "We'd better get going."

"Is it that late already?"

Sitting in the passenger seat of Sophia's SUV, Julie watched the town of White Birch slide past her view. Her heart leaped when she saw Ethan step out of his silver Honda.

Ethan! Hi. He looked handsome. She loved the way his coat hung straight from his square shoulders and how his slightly gelled brown waves glistened in the morning light.

She jerked her purse onto her lap and dug for her cell phone. *Did he get my note? Did I miss his call?*

After a second, she tossed her cell back into her purse.

"He didn't call?" Sophia asked in a low tone.

"No."

"Clod."

"Stop, Sophia. He's not a clod."

"OK, cad."

"Stop."

෨

"So the inspectors are bothering you," Grandpa said, cutting his pancakes in long strips and loading them up with butter and syrup.

"Does Grandma know you eat like this?" Ethan motioned with his fork at the syrup and buttered pancakes.

Grandpa smirked. "What, you think I'd do this behind her back?"

Ethan laughed. "She'd find out for sure, knowing this town."

"I imagine you're right."

"If you had a coronary, I was worried I'd have to out you. But if she knows—"

Grandpa speared his first bite. "I told her on my way to meet you, 'I'm having Sam's pancakes.'"

Ethan squirted ketchup on his pile of scrambled eggs.

"Those inspectors are about to give me a coronary."

"Just oblige them, son. It will make life easier."

"You'd think in this day and age a man would never hear the words 'in triplicate,' but it's standard op for those guys."

"Your dad struggled with them until he retired."

Ethan spread a thin coat of jam on his unbuttered wheat toast. "Yeah, when I asked him about it, he laughed."

"Might just be why he retired early."

"That or Mom getting on his case about working so hard." Growing up, Ethan often overheard his parents discussing his father's devotion to the business. Many times, his mother reasoned for more time at home and family vacations. His father talked about responsibility, loyalty, and hard work.

It was his father who masterminded the production process Ethan now managed. The implementation of his ideas rocketed Grandpa's small furniture business into a multimillion-dollar furniture factory.

Grandpa sipped his coffee. "He and your mom are having fun with their little tax business. Your dad always was good with numbers."

"It's a great second career for him. Keeps them busy in the winter so they can vacation the rest of the year."

The waitress came over with a coffeepot in each hand. "Heat up your coffee, Matt?"

Grandpa lifted his cup to her. "Janet, you've waited on me for over ten years. You know the answer."

"Sam makes me ask." She winked at the older man. "How about you, Ethan?"

"Decaf."

Janet poured from the orange-lipped pot in her left hand. "Can I get you anything else?"

Grandpa held up his fork. "I'll have another round of pancakes."

Ethan glanced up at Janet. "He tells me Grandma knows about his eating habits."

She laughed. "I'm sure she does. I'll put in the order."

Grandpa sat back and patted his flat belly. "Your grandma knows everything I do. It's our code."

Ethan furrowed his brow. "Your code?"

"Lambert's Code. I'll tell you about it some time. You're 'bout due, I think."

"I've never heard of Lambert's Code."

"It's one of the marriage rules your grandma and I live by. Just might help you and Julie along the way."

Ethan bent over his breakfast wondering if Grandpa could read the concern of his soul through his eyes. He'd never heard of Lambert's Code, but if it helped Grandpa's marriage to Grandma, he wanted to know.

"Want to tell me about it, Ethan?" grandpa interrupted his thoughts.

Ethan looked up. He regarded his grandpa's lean face, the one that had seen a great war, the one that had built a great business, and the one that knew great love. "Not sure I can put words to it."

"Work or home?"

"Home." The sole word spoke volumes.

Grandpa nodded, understanding without a word.

Ethan set his fork down and gazed out the diner window. The White Birch horizon promised sunshine. "We're snapping at each other, miscommunicating. We don't connect anymore."

"Consider the last few years, trying to start a family. Doctor visits, medical expenses, going to school, launching your careers. It's a lot to bear, Ethan."

Ethan's eyes burned for the first time in a long, long time. "I guess you're right. So tell me about this code you and Grandma invented."

"Well, I'll tell you—"

"Excuse me."

Ethan glanced up to see Dr. Patterson standing by the table, his hand extended.

"Dr. Patterson, good to see you." Ethan shook his hand.

The gentlemanly doctor greeted Grandpa Matt, then asked

Ethan, "Could I speak to you for a moment?"

Grandpa scooted out of the booth. "I think I'll find Sam and compliment his pancakes."

Dr. Patterson slid into his place. "I just wanted to remind you, these things are always hard."

Ethan rubbed his chin. "What things?" He didn't like the way the light faded from the good doctor's face.

"Did you talk to your wife yesterday?"

"Yes." *Sort of.*

Dr. Patterson regarded Ethan for a second. He started to say something when Grandpa returned.

"Janet's about to bring out my cakes. Is it safe?"

Dr. Patterson laughed and gave Grandpa his seat back. "I never get between a man and his breakfast."

"You're a good man, Casey."

Ethan felt unnerved, unsure what had prompted this odd, private conversation.

Dr. Patterson rapped his knuckles on the tabletop. "Ethan, why don't you stop by my office at twelve thirty?"

He nodded. "Okay."

"Nice to see you, Matt. Give my best to Betty."

Grandpa shook his hand. "Will do."

Ethan watched him leave, a gnawing feeling in the pit of his stomach.

five

"All right, class, settle down." Julie walked the breadth of the music room, passing out the graded short essays to her sixth graders. "Overall, very good work. May I suggest a review of your grammar rules?"

A collective moan filled the room. Julie laughed. *Groaners.* She taught a bunch of groaners. They groaned when she told them to practice, groaned when she gave them assignments. Yet despite the groans, she cared deeply for each of them.

She was about to move on to the day's music lesson when her classroom door opened and Ethan filled the doorway.

"Can I see you outside?" Only his lips moved; his jaw remained tight.

In the hall, Ethan did not greet her with a kiss or hello. "Were you planning on telling me that we can't have kids, or were you going to wait 'til we're fifty and say, 'Oh, by the by, Ethan, on that kid thing? Never gonna happen.'" He popped the wall with his fist.

A chill ran down Julie's back. "How did you find out?"

"Dr. Patterson, who else?"

"What? How?"

"I ran into him at the diner this morning. By the way, I wanted to take *you* to breakfast."

"How was I supposed to know?" Julie modulated her voice. Her words felt hard and brittle. "You could have told me you wanted to have breakfast."

Ethan stood right in front of her. "You could have told me, too, about the test results."

She focused on her shoes. "I couldn't find the words."

"Couldn't find the words? I'm your husband. Remember me, Jules, the man you vowed to cherish your whole life?"

34

She jerked her head up, eyes intent on Ethan. "Yes, and remember me, the woman you vowed to cherish your whole life?"

Ethan stood back, arms akimbo. "What are you saying? I don't cherish you?"

"I think I have stiff competition." There, she said it.

"Competition? With whom?" Ethan spread his arms, defensive, inviting conflict.

"Not whom. What." Julie counted off on her fingers. "Basketball, golf, football, racquetball, ice hockey. If it rolls, slides, bounces, or spirals, you give attention to it."

He huffed. "You're jealous of sports? I've always played sports. We *met* on the high school football field."

"Don't make me sound petty and stupid, Ethan. You know what I mean. You play or watch sports seven days a week. If it's not sports, it's work."

"And what about you? Music doesn't consume you?"

"No, not like sports consumes you."

"Having a child consumed—"

She gasped. He stopped, a contorted expression on his face. "Is that what you think? Really?"

He regarded her with his hands buried in his pockets. "It got to be a little consuming, I guess, at times, to be honest."

"Why didn't you say something? I thought we were making the decisions together, Ethan." She trembled with the reality of their conversation.

"I couldn't stand to—"

Snickers billowed from the classroom. Julie whirled around to find the door wide open, her class of sixth graders absorbing every word.

Horrified, she commanded, "Back to your seats." She shut the door with a bang and whipped around to Ethan. "Now see what you've done?"

"Don't blame me. You're the one with all the secrets. I suppose Sophia knows."

"She does not." Julie crossed her arms. "Can we talk about this later?"

"Later? What time would be convenient for you?" Ethan walked away.

"Please, don't go away mad. I planned to tell you today." Julie stepped toward him, touching his sleeve with the tips of her fingers.

Ethan faced his wife. "I'm not mad. I'm hurt and confused, Julie. You had all night to tell me."

She felt her heart lock down and couldn't form an answer.

He continued, "All you needed to say was, 'Ethan, we need to talk about something serious.' Instead, you get me in an argument about buying a new car."

She let her gaze fall on him. "I couldn't make myself say the words, 'I'm barren.'"

Ethan sighed as he walked toward her and pulled her to him. "I'm sorry, babe. I'm so sorry."

Julie rested her chin on his shoulder and cried a little, but most of her tears had already been shed.

"I'd better get back to class." She backed away. "I'll see you tonight."

"I thought we could go out tonight, the Italian Hills." He brushed her hair away from her face.

"Oh, Eth, that place is—"

"Jules?" He tugged on her hand, his brown eyes pleading.

"No, I can't. I just can't."

20

Ethan shut the door to his office and whirled his desk chair around. He snatched up the production reports, his thoughts a million miles away.

Crash! Ethan peered over the desk's edge. *Perfect, just perfect.* His favorite coffee mug lay shattered on the hardwood floor.

As he swept up the last shard, Will rapped lightly on the door's glass window. Ethan motioned for him to come in.

"Everything okay in here?"

"In here, yes. With my wife, no." The residue of his conversation with Julie coated his emotions—frustration mingled with ire, compassion with sadness.

"Ah, I see." Will's voice contained the proper amount of understanding, but Ethan knew he would not probe further.

Lambert's Furniture was a place of business, not a counseling center. Will ran a family-oriented company, but he wouldn't take business time to untangle Ethan's marriage knots.

"Did you e-mail me those warehouse construction estimates?" Will asked.

Ethan meant to do that after their nine o'clock meeting, but the prospect of meeting with Dr. Patterson, and an issue with the new product line, distracted him.

"On their way right now." Ethan fished through his in-box for the contractor estimates.

"Okay, thanks." Will shut the door behind him as he exited. Ethan found the e-mails and forwarded them to Will's address.

Julie, what's happening to us?

He found it hard to concentrate on his afternoon tasks. Normally, the day-to-day routine calmed him, even on his worst days. He liked the feeling that some things never changed.

But the confrontation with Julie caused him to cringe. He shouldn't have infused the situation with his anger and embarrassed her in front of her students. He'd only added insult to injury.

"Lord, forgive me." With decisive motion, Ethan dialed his wife's cell. She would be in class, but he planned on leaving a humble message.

"Julie, I'm sorry I went to the school upset and angry. Please, let's go to the Italian Hills. We can have a nice romantic dinner and talk, okay? Bye, babe."

He hung up, feeling better but unable to escape his restlessness. He stared out the window for a minute, thinking, watching the narrow rays of the sun moving westward.

Then he knew what he wanted to do. He shot a quick e-mail to Will.

Gone for the rest of the day. Call my cell if you need me. See you in the morning. Ethan

Ten minutes later, he walked under the shadows of the covered bridge, whispering prayers to his heavenly Father like the wind whispering under the eaves.

❧

Julie followed the Italian Hills maître d' to a candlelit table under the western window where snow powdered the windowsill.

Ethan held her chair as she sat down. "Isn't this great, babe? Fantastic food, romantic atmosphere, you and me."

Julie smiled at him, attempting to appreciate his efforts to smooth a healing balm over the wound of the day. *Think of something nice to say.* "They do have good food." She regarded her husband as he scanned the menu. He looked like a kid poring over a Christmas toy catalog.

She resolved to enjoy herself, or at least pretend to for Ethan's sake. He was trying to fix things between them after all.

But the Italian Hills' amorous atmosphere made her feel like an alien. How could she wander down the dreamy path of romance when her heart still lingered in the valley of the shadow of death?

Oh Lord. . .

"Are you having the usual?" Ethan peeked over his menu, the flame of the candle flickering in his brown eyes.

Julie glanced at the entrée section. Items that used to make her mouth water now made her stomach churn. "I'm not terribly hungry."

"Not hungry for portabella pasta?" He motioned at the waiter passing by. "Could we get some bread here?"

The young man answered with a slight bow. "I'll get your server."

"Mercy, Ethan. Are you that hungry? Wait for our server to come over."

"Yes, I'm that hungry," he retorted.

Silence lingered as they decided their order. When the server brought their bread and took their drink order, Ethan commented, "You look beautiful, Julie."

"Thank you." Ethan was charming yet sincere; Julie wondered how he managed to find the weakness in her emotional barriers time and time again.

He looked equally as handsome in his white mock turtleneck and navy slacks, but she couldn't form the words. He knew, didn't he, after all these years?

"So how're we doing tonight?" Ethan leaned over the table toward her.

"*We* are fine."

He took her hand in his. "I'm really sorry about today, babe. I was out of line."

She bowed her head. "I'm sorry, too, Ethan. I wanted to tell you, but just—"

"I understand. It's okay."

"Oh, Ethan, what are we going to do? All my life, I've—"

"Ethan. Julie. Hi." Julie swerved to see Ethan's cousin, Elizabeth Donovan, and her husband, Kavan, approaching.

"Good evening, you two." Ethan stood to greet them, glancing down at Julie with a what-do-we-do-now face.

"Would you like to join them?" the maître d' asked, a server already moving another two-top table over.

"That would be lovely. Do you mind?" Elizabeth smiled at them. "We've been wanting to get together with you two."

"Same here," Ethan said halfheartedly.

But not tonight, Julie thought. How could they chitchat with Elizabeth and Kavan when they had so much to discuss? Would it be rude to ask them to sit someplace else? Surely they would understand.

But the table was set, Elizabeth and Kavan were seated, and the server headed for the kitchen with their drink order.

Ethan touched her leg with his foot under the table to get her attention. His eyes pleaded with her. She smiled with a nod.

They never should have gone out to dinner. She hated the feeling of *I told you so*, but he'd insisted, forgetting that a Lambert in White Birch, New Hampshire, was like a magnet.

Everywhere a Lambert goes, another Lambert is sure to show.

So they had company for dinner. It took every ounce of Julie's energy to engage in small talk with Elizabeth while Kavan and Ethan discussed something she couldn't quite hear. Any other day, any other time, they would have treasured Elizabeth and Kavan's company, but tonight, oh, not tonight. The casual conversation only added to the heaviness of her soul.

In short order, their server set down a round of iced teas and a basket of hot bread. Ethan buttered a hot slice and asked Kavan, "So what brings you and Elizabeth here night?"

The young couple beamed at each other, holding back enormous grins, or so it seemed to Julie.

"Well, we're celebrating." Elizabeth's smile lit her face.

"We could ask the same of you," Kavan interjected, reaching for the butter plate. "What are you two doing here?"

Julie peered into Ethan's eyes as if to anchor her turbulent emotions.

Ethan coughed and stumbled over his words, but finally said, "Nothing special, just a nice dinner." He buttered another slice of bread, though the first one remained uneaten.

Julie ached to change the topic away from her and Ethan. Didn't Elizabeth say they were celebrating? Perhaps she got a raise or promotion at Creager.

"How's your job at Creager?" Julie asked Elizabeth with a hint of enthusiasm.

"Great, actually." Elizabeth sipped her tea. "I'm still in awe of how the Lord led me to that company. It's way more fun than grad school."

"We make our plans, but the Lord directs our steps," Ethan quoted from Proverbs.

"The pay is better than grad school." Kavan winked at his wife. "She makes a lot more than I do."

Elizabeth laughed. "That will all change soon, Kavan."

"I know, but let me relish having a rich wife for a moment."

Julie squirmed in her seat, feeling as if the world were

closing in around her. She was about to excuse herself for the ladies' room when the server brought their salads.

Ethan prayed for the food, and when they echoed his amen, he asked, "So, Beth, what's going to change soon? You're not leaving your job, are you?"

In her peripheral vision, Julie saw Elizabeth catch her husband's gaze.

"Should we tell them?" she whispered.

Kavan grinned. "Some things are meant to be celebrated, honey." He tapped his fork against the side of his tea glass. "We have an announcement."

"Let's hear it, man." Ethan clapped his cousin-in-law on the back.

Julie's stomach knotted. *No, Ethan, let's not hear it.*

Kavan motioned for Elizabeth to do the honors. "Well, we weren't expecting this." She tucked a strand of her curly brown hair behind her ear. "But. . .we're *expecting*."

Kavan burst with laughter. "Elizabeth, pregnant. Can you believe it?" He toasted her with his glass of iced tea.

Ethan coughed. "Congrat—Congratulations." He wiped the edge of his lips with his napkin with a covert glance at Julie.

Elizabeth reached across the table for Kavan's hand. "My life has been all about change and hanging on to God this past year and a half, but this moves me to a whole new level."

"We weren't planning on it so soon." Kavan stopped as the server set down another round of iced teas.

Elizabeth shook her head. "Last month, the idea of being a mom freaked me out. But this month we decided, it's happening. Let's celebrate and tell people." She laughed. "A baby. Our very own baby."

"Julie?" Ethan nudged his wife. "Isn't this great?"

Julie shook all over and deep in her inner being. "Excuse me." She pushed away from the table and fled the restaurant.

six

"Well, what did you want me to say? 'Oh, that's terrible? We can't have kids, so why should you?'" Ethan paced the length of their bedroom, one hand on the back of his neck, the other on his hip.

"Of course not." Julie lifted her face from the pillow. Black mascara covered her high cheekbones, and her green eyes were swollen.

"Then what do you want from me?" Ethan faced her, his arms spread.

She opened her mouth but lost her words to a deep, gut-wrenching sob.

Ethan sighed. "Jules, you've got to stop crying. We'll never get anywhere otherwise." He sat on the edge of the bed, his hand on her leg.

She jerked away from his touch. Ethan fell back on the bed. "Don't be this way. We're in this together, aren't we?"

"I don't know; are we?" Julie slid off the bed, unzipped her dress, and dropped it to the floor.

Ethan could see her arms and hands trembling. All this, and they still had yet to discuss, heart to heart, the curveball life had just thrown them.

He decided to take a different approach. "Do you want to talk to Dr. Patterson together? He recommended meeting with him."

"Why? It's not going to change anything." Julie ducked into the bathroom. Ethan heard the water running in the sink.

"He's experienced, walked other couples through this. He understands the last few years have been difficult for us."

She leaned out the bathroom door, toothbrush in her hand. "So sorry to have been an inconvenience to you."

Ethan lowered his head. "Did I say that? I said us, Julie, us."

She shut the door.

This is going nowhere fast. Ethan got up and changed his clothes.

"Are you going to leave your dress and slip in the middle of the floor?" he asked his wife when she emerged from the bathroom.

Julie picked up her clothes and dropped them on the bedside rocking chair. "Happy?" She crawled into bed with one eye on Ethan.

"Julie, I'm not the bad guy here." Ethan draped his shirt over a hanger.

"Too bad you'll never pass on your neat-freak genes to some poor unsuspecting child."

"Too bad you won't be able to create another slob." As soon as he spoke the words, Ethan regretted them.

"Jules, I'm sorry." But it was too late. She'd burrowed under the covers.

❧

Julie woke with a start, shivering. For a moment or two, she felt lost in the cold darkness, unable to discern her surroundings. Her head and eyes ached. Squinting, she read the time from the bedside clock.

Two o'clock in the morning.

Then, like waking up from a peaceful sleep into a nightmare, she remembered the night before. Dinner at Italian Hills. Elizabeth and Kavan having a baby. The horrid exchange with Ethan. And the tears, the river of tears. She was so weary of tears.

She scooted toward Ethan's side of the bed, her hand outstretched. But the sheets and pillow were cold and empty.

"Eth?"

No response.

She called again, louder. "Ethan?"

Tossing the blankets aside, Julie scurried to the bathroom for her robe. A wintry chill hovered in the room.

She eased down the stairs and made her way through the apartment by the dim glow of light that filtered through the drawn verticals. Pausing briefly, she peered out to see it snowing again.

"Ethan?" She peeked around the den door. Ethan lay curled and cold on the short sofa. "Oh, babe—"

Fumbling for the closet door, Julie patted around the shelves for a spare blanket. From its scent, she could tell it was the one they used for fall picnics in Milo Park.

She buried her face in the blanket and tried to remember the last time they'd actually picnicked together. Two years ago?

Spreading the cover over her husband now, Julie thought it odd, yet wonderful, that the old blanket still carried the fragrance of Saturday afternoons in the park.

Shivering, she wriggled onto the edge of the couch, fitting next to Ethan. He stirred and scooted over to make room for her. Curling his arm around her waist, he kissed her softly on the nape of her neck.

In a moment or two, Julie drifted to sleep, Ethan's warmth melting away the chill of the night.

∂≈

Friday night, Ethan parked along the curb of Wiltshire Street beneath the bright lights of the Hanover home. He turned to Julie. "Let's miss this one."

"We'd never hear the end of it." She pulled on her door handle.

"A hundred of their soirees and you'd think we'd get a reprieve from one." Ethan caught her hand. "Say the word, and we leave."

"You say that every time." She cupped his cheek with the palm of her hand.

"I mean it every time."

Snow crunched under his feet as he stepped out of the car into the orange glow of the streetlights. Ethan followed the lights' hue to the edge of the driveway where Julie waited.

Without a word, she started up the steep drive, but Ethan

stopped her with his touch on her coat sleeve. "Wait, Julie."

When she faced him, his heartbeat echoed in his ears. "You look amazing tonight."

Her smile challenged the moon's glow. "Thank you."

He brushed her coat sleeve with his hand. "Let's phone in our apology and go eat pizza. We can get a corner in the back, talk, kiss."

She smoothed her hand over his chest. "Give it a rest, Ethan. This routine is getting old."

"*This* routine is getting old." He motioned toward the Hanover's triple-story home, then drew her to him. Her scent made him think of beauty and kindness. "Think about it, Jules. Snobby society people, your mom suggesting you change your hair, your dad introducing you to violin players." He made a face.

She laughed. "Violin players do have their purpose, darling. Don't be a complete cello snob."

He kissed her. "Since Tuesday, we've been out every night this week: church on Wednesday, private lessons on Thursday."

"I'm used to it."

Ethan drew back. "Used to what?"

"You going one way, me the other."

"All the more reason to skip this shindig."

"Perhaps you could skip a ball game."

Ethan lifted his arms. He was out of words. "Yeah, whatever; that'll fix it."

Julie snapped, "You might as well tell me my opinion doesn't count, Ethan."

"Let's just go inside. I'm tired of debating."

"Fine with me."

The front door opened. Sandy Hanover graced the porch, elegant in a black dress and a string of pearls. "Come in, you two. You'll catch cold out here."

"We're coming." Julie waved like all was right with the world.

Ethan stepped in front of her. "Julie, sooner or later we have to talk about our life and what's next."

Julie peered into the dark shadows beyond the Hanovers' front yard. "Yes, I know." She started up the drive again.

Ethan fell in stride. "We can't keep diffusing the issue with frivolous arguments. Half the time we don't even know what we're arguing about."

With that, Julie stopped. "Do you want to talk about it? I'm barren. There, we've discussed it. End of the issue."

Ethan balked. "We haven't discussed it at all." He paused. "Julie," he said, firm and resolute, "pizza. Let's go for pizza."

Ralph Hanover came out this time. "Julie, Kit Merewether is inside. She's eager to talk with you."

Julie glanced at Ethan. "Can we do what I want for a change, without a big brouhaha?"

"Brouhaha? What brouhaha? I want an evening with my wife to discuss our future."

She sighed. "Ethan, I'm going inside. You can come if you want."

He rubbed his gloved hand over his head and followed.

❧

Music and laughter warmed the room. Julie maneuvered her way to the buffet, feeling like an ice cube among burning coals. She thanked her mother when she handed her a hot cup of tea.

"Are you well?" Mom asked, brushing her hand over Julie's forehead.

Julie pulled away. "Yes, I'm fine."

Kit Merewether joined them with a broad smile. "Julie, you're as lovely as ever."

"Thank you, Kit." Julie let the older woman link their arms and drag her away to meet the newest members of New Hampshire's elite orchestra.

Kit introduced Julie to a small circle with a great deal of enthusiasm. "She won the George Houston Musical Fellowship," Kit concluded, beaming as if she herself had given birth to Julie Hanover Lambert.

"Congratulations."

"What was the focus of your fellowship study?"

Julie told them, "Bringing the classics back into the elementary and secondary school level."

From another room, Julie heard a roar of *yeahs!*

"Golf," someone said.

Without looking, Julie figured Ethan was among that crowd. In fact, he probably inspired the idea of watching the game. No matter where or what, her husband found a home watching sports.

Kit shook her gray head, her expression one of amusement. "One would think it better than rocket science, or the melodies of Brahms, for a man to knock a small round ball into a small round hole."

A laugh rose from the circle. "One would think."

Kit inquired of Julie, "Will you battle Ethan over the value of music versus the value of sports for your children? Certainly you will."

The room faded to shades of gray. Kit didn't know, of course. But like a moth to the flame, Julie's mother flitted over at the mention of children.

"We were talking about Julie's children. Shall they learn to putt a tiny white ball or the fine art of playing the cello?"

Sandy Hanover brushed Julie's hair from her face. "Probably both." She smiled at Kit. "Julie and Ethan's children will be beautiful, talented, and take the world by storm."

Julie coughed. "Does it really matter?"

Mom rested her hand at the base of her throat. "Of course it matters." She moved her other hand to Kit's arm. "At the age of five, Julie lined up all of her dolls and taught them 'Jesus Loves Me,' and I don't know what all."

Turning to Julie, she asked, "Do you remember your little doll choir?"

Julie nodded. "But I don't think it means my children will be brilliant. I think it means my dolls couldn't protest."

Kit peered at Julie with a raised brow, but Julie looked away.

Her probing gray eyes might unearth a bomb Julie did not want exposed.

"Her father and I wanted more children, but—"

Julie touched her mother's shoulder. "We all know, Mom."

A server with a tray of punch paused at their trio. Sandra Hanover picked up a cup. "Nevertheless, we expect to hear we are going to be grandparents anytime now."

Kit took a cup, but Julie declined, gripping her hands together at her waist.

"How long have you two been married?" Kit asked.

"Ten years this summer."

Sandra sipped her punch, then told Kit, "They virtually dragged both families to the church the summer after graduation."

"Young lovers, I see." Kit's words were simple and few, but Julie felt the revelation of them. Yes, they were young and in love.

"We met on the high school football field. A fourth and goal play knocked Ethan out, and when they called for smelling salts, I ran onto the field." Julie stuck her arm in the air. "Nurse Julie."

Kit's deep, pure laugh billowed around them.

Julie's mom laughed a little too heartily and finished the tale Sandra Hanover style, waving her hands. "Ethan came to, looked at his nurse, and got knocked out again."

"With love," Kit concluded. "The world's most powerful potion."

Sandy flipped her hand in the air as if it were no big deal. "So you see, Kit, we've been waiting to be grandparents for almost ten years."

"Well, well." Kit looked at Julie as if she could read all her secret thoughts. "Grandchildren are always a blessing."

"Ralph already set up a trust account, two of them, as a matter of fact. He didn't want to wait." Julie's mom chortled, pressing her hand on Kit's arm. "Julie and Ethan will have a time keeping us from spoiling them."

"Leave it to a finance lawyer to think ahead," Kit said.

Julie squirmed, Kit's piercing gaze bore right through her. She glanced around to avoid eye contact and caught the back of Ethan's head in the family room, where, sure enough, he hovered around the golf game.

"But you chose to get an education, Julie?" Kit tipped her head and raised a brow.

"Yes, she and Ethan both earned their degrees," Sandy Hanover answered for her.

My mother, the broadcaster. Julie squared her shoulders and said to Kit, "We wanted children right away, but I miscarried our first year of marriage. We took a long look at things and realized we weren't very well prepared, financially, emotionally—"

"Spiritually," Kit interjected.

"Yes, of course." Julie knew Kit to be a wise, godly woman. And tonight she seemed to have a direct line to her heart. "We decided to wait."

"Well, the waiting is over. I want to Christmas shop for my grandchildren." Mom said the words with an air of finality, as if saying them would make it true.

Julie's stomach knotted. "I hear you, Mom."

"Hasn't Dr. Patterson worked his wonders yet?"

Treading on tender ground, Mom. "God is the God of wonders, Mom. Dr. Patterson is limited to what man can do."

"I tell you, if such things had been available to your father and me—"

"Mom!"

She faced Julie with a sharp turn. "I don't appreciate your tone, Julie."

"Julie," Kit interjected. "I'm forming a quartet. Please say you'll join us. We need an outstanding cellist." Her comment diffused the moment.

"A quartet? I thought of auditioning for the symphony—"

Kit touched her arm. "Join our quartet. You'll have more fun, and it'll give you something to look forward to."

seven

Ethan liked Steve Tripleton, a friend of Julie's father, with his over-the-top confidence and successful businessman bravado. He could do without the designer slacks and Italian loafers, but otherwise Ethan found Steve engaging.

"We'll go down to Costa Rica mid-April. Heredia has a beautiful golf resort. Absolutely beautiful."

Ethan rubbed his hands together. Golfing in the Caribbean, sun on his back, warm breeze in his face. . . For the first time all night, he was glad to be at the Hanovers'. "Sounds like my kind of trip. How much, Steve?"

"For five days? Around fifteen hundred, give or take. That'd cover your flight, accommodations, green fees. You'd need a little spending money for food and incidentals."

Very reasonable. Ethan mentally reviewed their finances— current savings balance plus whatever he could add in the next month after paying their monthly bills. *I can swing it, I think. Still have all summer to save a down payment for Julie's car.*

"I'm game," her father said. "Winter is wearing me down. I think the office can do without me for a few days."

Steve clapped him on the back, his smile exposing overly white teeth. "You have the Internet? We can get online and take a tour."

"Right this way." Ralph headed for his upstairs office.

Ethan followed, offering ideas and suggestions. "I think my cousin Will Adams might want to come along."

"Ethan."

He turned to see Julie at the bottom of the stairs. He leaned over the railing. "Yeah, babe, what's up?"

In a low voice, she said, "I'm ready to go."

He hesitated. "Okay, give me a minute. I'm checking on

something with your dad and Steve."

Her father called down from the mezzanine. "Julie, Eliza set up a grand smorgasbord fit for a king. Did you try her shrimp puffs?"

Julie gave him a thin smile, her hands clasped at her waist. "I had my heart set on pizza."

At that, Ethan responded, "Finally saw it my way?"

"Whatever, Eth. Let's go."

"Five minutes." He dashed upstairs. He didn't want Steve to get too far ahead on the virtual tour.

A little while later, when Ethan strolled out of the office with Steve and Ralph, visions of blue green seas and lush lawns danced in his head.

"I'll get my secretary on the arrangements. Ethan, speak to your cousin. A foursome would be nice."

"Done." Ethan flipped Steve his card. "Here are my numbers, cell, work, and home."

At the bottom of the stairs, he remembered Julie. A quick peek at his watch told him five minutes had turned to thirty.

"See you gentlemen later. I need to find my wife."

Ethan mingled among the crowd, searching for Julie. Sandy caught him and reminded him it was not too late to give her a grandchild by Christmas.

He blushed and said, "Sure, Sandy."

Eliza tried to entice him with a plate of food, but he wanted to save room for pizza, the one junk food he enjoyed.

He found Kit Merewether by the fireplace in a lively small-group discussion.

"Pardon me," he interrupted, popping into the group, addressing Kit. "Have you seen Julie?"

"No, I haven't, dear."

"She left," someone said.

Ethan turned around. "Do you know when?"

"Twenty minutes ago, maybe?"

Ethan jerked his coat from under the pile on the bed in the guest room. Without saying good-bye, he stepped into the cold night and strode with purpose toward his car.

But it was gone.

⋙

At a booth in the back of Giuseppe's Pizza, Julie shoved aside the remains of a large house salad and sipped on a diet soda.

She twisted the paper straw wrapper between her fingers, wondering if Ethan would show.

"She's a-waiting for you. Back here." The sound of Giuseppe's voice neared.

Ethan slipped into the booth across from her with a quick thanks to the round-bellied proprietor. "Do you want to tell me why you left?" He shrugged off his coat, his face red from the cold.

"Did you walk here?" She swirled the ice in her soda glass and took a long drink.

"Yes, I needed to cool off."

"You're mad then."

He leaned toward her. "I asked you to wait."

"I told you I wanted to leave."

"Five minutes. All I wanted was five minutes."

Julie tapped the face of her watch. "Yet here it is, an hour later."

He reclined against the padded booth. "I'm sorry. I got interested in something."

"What? Sports? Why is that always more important than I am?"

"That's unfair. And not true. What happened anyway? Why did you want to leave?"

She leaned toward him. With a clipped tone, she said, "My mother."

He winced. " 'Nuff said. Sorry, babe."

"She went on and on to Kit Merewether about *her* grand-children." She wiped her nose with the tip of a wadded-up napkin. "She told her about Dad's bank accounts for them."

"Yeah, she cornered me about giving them a grandchild by Christmas."

"Let's not tell them, Ethan. Please."

He shook his head, a wry grin on his lips. "We have to tell them eventually."

A skinny, squeaky-voiced teenager stopped and crouched at their table. He set his elbows on the table, his pen poised over the order pad. "Can I get you something to drink?"

"Coffee," Ethan said. "A big mug."

"I'll take a hot tea this time." Julie slid her empty soda glass across the table.

"Bring us a large cheese pie, too." Ethan ordered.

Julie looked into Ethan's eyes. "There's no little Ethan or little Julie in our future. Does it bother you?" To her surprise, verbalizing her thoughts comforted her heart.

He reached for her hand. "Yes, it bothers me."

With her head down, she confessed, "I can't stop thinking about it. The idea lives with me. I've let you down."

"Let me down? No, you haven't, babe."

"I feel betrayed by my own body. I've let you down, Mom and Dad. Your parents."

With his fingertips, Ethan lifted her chin so she faced him. "Don't carry this burden yourself, Julie. We are in this together. For better or worse."

"Then why do I feel so alone?"

"Because you exclude me. I had to hear the news from Dr. Patterson. Does that seem right to you?"

The waiter brought their drinks and a basket of garlic knots. Ethan reached for one.

"I don't know what seems right to me anymore."

"We're going to figure this out. We just need time to think, and talk."

"And pray. Ethan, what is God saying in all of this?"

He shrugged, his eyes fixed on some point beyond her. "I wish I knew. But He's faithful. He has a plan and a purpose, babe."

"I cling to that, or I'd give up completely," Julie said. She watched him for a moment and then asked, "What'd Jesse say about my car?"

"It was your starter. He fixed it, good as new."

"Good as new. Ha! I want a new car, Ethan."

Ethan swigged his coffee. "A new car isn't going to take away the pain, Julie."

"I didn't say it would." Julie chewed her lower lip, wondering what would make the pain go away.

"You know our financial situation. Adding a monthly car payment would really strap us."

When their large cheese pizza arrived, Julie took a plate and a large slice of pizza. "So it's my fault I don't have a new car?"

Ethan sighed. She understood he was frustrated, but she didn't care. So was she.

"Did I say that? We decided together to continue seeking medical help, didn't we?"

"You agreed after pressure from me and my parents."

He nodded. "Yes, but I wouldn't have agreed if I didn't think it was the right decision."

Julie wondered for the first time how much her parents' desire for a child had impacted her and Ethan's decisions.

"It's seems if I can't have a baby, I should at least get a new car."

"Jules, those two things are mutually exclusive." He reached across and squeezed her hand. "We'll get you a new car."

"Tomorrow."

"No, not tomorrow."

❧

Saturday morning, Ethan slept until eleven. He loved that about the weekend—sleeping in. Half awake, he rolled over to snuggle Julie.

But he found her side of the bed empty. "Jules?"

He waited a moment for her answer. "Julie?" When she didn't respond, he crawled out of bed.

Cold air permeated the apartment as he jogged downstairs. "Jules?"

"In here."

He found her in the den, curled in the recliner, Bible propped open in her lap, her expression somber. His heart yearned for her. "Hey, sweetie, what's going on?"

He scooped her up and sat down, cradling her in his lap. He kissed her softly when she dropped her head against his shoulder.

"I was just talking to the Lord about our situation."

He brushed her hair away from her face. "Did He say anything?"

Julie shook her head. "Why does He seem so silent when I need Him the most?"

Ethan wondered the same thing. He wished he knew the answer, but his own prayer life lacked luster these days. His list of excuses seemed more and more frivolous, but he had yet to adjust the situation. He knew they could trust Him, believe in Him, even when they didn't understand their life circumstance. "Remember what I said last night? He's faithful, Julie. He has a plan and a purpose."

"I know He works all things together for good. I just can't find the good here." She cried, wiping her face with wadded tissues. "Will you pray with me?"

"Absolutely." He rested his cheek on the top of her head, regretting that she had to ask him to pray. He should have offered.

"Lord, we don't understand this situation, but You do. We can count on Your faithfulness, Your goodness, Your blessings. Give us grace to submit to Your will for our lives."

For the first time in a long time, Ethan sensed the presence and peace of God. They stirred a hunger in him and a resolve to seek the Lord's strength and stop depending on his own devices.

After a peaceful interlude, Julie pressed her lips against his cheek. "Thank you."

"Do you feel better? Do you sense the Lord's peace?"

She nodded slightly. "Yes. I know He loves me, but, Ethan, I don't know if I'll ever feel better."

He frowned at her. "That's my beautiful little pessimist."

She flicked him on the forehead, grinning.

"Ouch!" He slapped his hand over the sting.

"That's what you get for being sarcastic." She kissed the red spot and hopped off his lap. "Do you want some breakfast? Your Highness slept until lunch, but I think I can whip up something breakfastlike for you."

"Eggs, please."

"Eggs it is." She smiled at him. "Thanks for praying with me." She disappeared around the corner to the kitchen.

He followed her. "You're welcome. Sorry you had to ask for prayer. I guess I've been a little dense lately."

"Just lately?" She snickered and retrieved the skillet from the bottom cupboard and sprayed it with cooking oil. "Can you believe we have a whole day with nothing to do?"

He slipped his hands around her waist. "Not me. I've got to run by the plant to check on the equipment." He nuzzled her neck.

"Really?" She faced him and slipped her arms around his neck.

He kissed her with passion.

"Let me guess. The eggs can wait."

"Maybe?" He searched her eyes, hoping to see a reflection of what he felt.

She returned his kiss without a word, then clicked off the burner and led him by the hand upstairs.

eight

Praying with Ethan lifted Julie's countenance and strengthened her resolve. *Move on with life. No more tears.*

Nevertheless, the word *barren* floated aimlessly along the breezes of her mind like tumbleweed across the desert plains.

She understood now, in some small way, what the apostle Paul meant when he wrote, "But one thing I do, forgetting those things which are behind and reaching forward to those things which are ahead."

With her life plans now defunct, new plans awaited. She merely needed to pray, dream, and let the Lord paint a new picture on the canvas of her life.

At the breakfast nook, she stared out the window at the glistening snow. *Time to give Kit Merewether a call and take her up on the quartet invitation.*

Ethan clattered around in the kitchen, putting away the breakfast dishes. "Kitchen is tidy, ready for your inspection, Mrs. Lambert." He bent to kiss her cheek.

The scent of mountain-spring soap drifted under her nose. "If it meets your standards, it meets mine."

Ethan lifted his arms over his head in a victory stance. "Ethan Lambert, Neat Freak Champion of the World."

She laughed at him. "Neat Freak, where's the paper? I want to catch up on the news. I feel out of touch."

"Probably on the porch. I'll get it."

The phone rang as he opened the front door. Still smiling, Julie answered.

"Hi, Julie, it's Mark Benton. Is Ethan around?"

"Hi, Mark. Hold on, here he is."

Julie handed the phone to her husband. He tossed her

the paper. Slowly she removed the plastic wrap, listening to Ethan's conversation.

He talked to Mark with animated movements—dribbling and shooting a pretend basketball. Julie perched on a nook stool and scouted out movies.

When he said good-bye to Mark, Ethan lobbed the phone to Julie. "Incoming. . ."

She caught it. "What's up?"

Ethan cupped her face in his hands and kissed her with enthusiasm. "A rematch. Mark ran into a couple of the guys from the Creager Technologies team, and they want a rematch of our championship game. Creager versus Lambert Furniture."

"Really. When?"

Ethan glanced at the stove clock. "Wow, is it that late? I've got to run by the plant, then get to this game." He dashed upstairs.

Julie trailed him. "What am I supposed to do?"

Ethan peeled off his sweater and jeans. "Come to the game." He folded the clothes and set them on top of his dresser.

"What about our free day?"

"Aw, babe, I have to check on the new CNC machines. I'm sorry I didn't tell you about that." He grabbed her and whirled her around. "But come to the game. It'll be fun." He disappeared in the closet for his basketball gear. "I can't believe those guys want to get beat again."

She flopped down on the bed. "I don't know. . ."

He slung his gym bag over his shoulder. "You can cheer me on."

She made a face and laughed. "You never hear me."

"It's the thought that counts." He ruffled her hair.

"And I lose my voice for nothing."

He looked at his watch. "Ooh, gotta go. Come on, Jules, come. Or, hey, call Elizabeth for a movie if you want."

"Well, I haven't talked to her since that night at the restaurant. I guess I could—" But he was gone.

Julie sat in the living room, acknowledging her sour attitude. She wanted to hang out at home with Ethan. He had to work and play basketball. So typical.

Work I understand, but basketball? She considered going to the game but didn't want to give Ethan the satisfaction.

When the phone rang a few minutes later, she answered, hoping to hear Ethan's voice.

"Do you want to catch a movie tonight?" Sophia sounded like an energetic teenager.

With a sigh, Julie leaned against the kitchen counter. "What a coincidence."

"Huh?"

"Never mind. Yeah, a movie sounds good."

"What do you want to see?" Sophia asked.

"I don't care as long as it's a comedy. The more inane, the better."

Sophia snickered. "That new place out by Sinclair's has eight theaters. I'm sure one of them is showing something inane."

"Great. Guess we could do dinner, too."

"Perfect."

Julie scribbled Ethan a note. *Gone to dinner and the movies with Sophia.* She tucked it under his laptop and bounded upstairs for a shower.

❧

Ethan knocked lightly on his grandparents' kitchen door. "Hello. Anyone home?" He wandered through the kitchen, snatching a piece of chocolate cake.

"Who's there?" Grandma came in from the family room with her knitting in her hands. "Ethan, what brings you here?"

"Stopped by to see my two favorite people." He bent to kiss her cheek.

Grandma chortled. "Have you had dinner?"

"Actually, no."

"Sit, sit. Let me get you something." Grandma set the yarn and needles on the kitchen counter and hustled around the airy kitchen.

"Where's Grandpa?" Ethan glanced through the kitchen door to the family room.

"Ratting around in the basement, making something, I think." With a Tupperware bowl in hand, Grandma opened the basement door. "Matt, Ethan is here."

Ethan heard footfalls on the stairs. "Well, to what do we owe this pleasure? Where's your lovely bride?"

"At a movie with a friend." Ethan watched as his grandpa hugged his grandma.

"How's *my* bride?" Grandpa kissed her and picked up the cake plate.

Bride? It had been many years since Ethan thought of Julie as his bride. Wife? Yes. Friend? Certainly. But bride? The word painted a different image on his emotions—an image of zealous love, of intimacy.

Grandma regarded Grandpa, a large spoon in her hand. "She's fine as long as you don't die too soon from cholesterol poisoning. Don't eat that whole cake, Matt."

"Ah, Betty, you worry too much." He fished in the silverware drawer for a fork and joined Ethan at the table.

Ethan watched, amused. His grandparents' enduring love and affection were a Lambert family treasure. Their example, along with his parents', gave him the confidence to marry Julie after high school. He had been blissfully unaware that desert winds would blow.

"What have you been doing today?" Grandpa scooted up to the table, a large white napkin tucked into his collar.

"Slept until noon, stopped by the plant to check on the equipment, then met the guys at the rec center to beat Creager again in a championship rematch."

"Those fellows must love punishment."

Ethan grinned. "They must."

"A lovely March Saturday and you went to work, played basketball, and Julie went out with a friend." Grandpa shook his head. "Times have sure changed."

Ethan narrowed his eyes. "What are you implying?"

Grandma came around the table. "All I had was leftover steak and baked beans from the senior center cookout." She patted him on the back and winked.

"Well, if that's all you have. . ." Ethan cut a bite. "I'll have to endure."

Grandpa lifted his chin. "When's the last time you and Julie went out together?"

Ethan thought for a moment. "Um. . ."

"Um? That doesn't sound good."

"Wait, we went to Italian Hills the other night." Ethan pointed at Grandpa with his fork. "She'd had a bad day." He left it at that.

"A consolation date?"

"No, not exactly." Ethan flushed and took a long sip of his water. "What's wrong with a consolation date?" *Never mind how rotten it was.*

"Nothing, if that's the kind of relationship you want with your wife. Are you two living life from the same game book?"

Ethan felt invaded by his grandpa's words. The man saw too much. "Where'd you come up with that? Game book? Of course we're living life from the same game book." *I think.*

"Would Julie tell me the same? Does she still drive that old car?"

Ethan squirmed. Grandpa painted him into a corner. "Yes."

"Matt, leave the boy alone. He and Julie can manage their own affairs." Grandma hushed Grandpa with a pat on the head.

"I never told you about Lambert's Code, did I?"

"Just that there was some mysterious family code." Ethan speared a piece of meat, grateful for Grandma's defense, shoving aside any guilt about Julie's old car. Two weeks ago, she happily drove that old car. How did the baby news change all that?

Grandma answered, "No mystery to it, Ethan. Just submit to one another."

Ethan gave her a quizzical look. "That's it?"

Grandma assured him, "That's it."

"Submit to one another?" Ethan repeated with a slight

shake of his head. "I have no idea what that means."

"Exactly." Grandpa speared the air with his fork. Cake crumbs littered the table.

"Matthew Lambert, you're worse than the great-grandchildren." Grandma got up for a wet cloth.

Ethan twisted his expression. "I'm supposed to live by a code I don't understand?"

"You've watched spy movies, haven't you?" Grandpa asked.

"Sure."

"Don't they crack some kind of code? That's what you have to do. Crack the code."

Grandma gave him a clue. "Read Ephesians 5:21."

"I know Ephesians 5. Husbands, love your wives. Wives, respect your husbands." He didn't say, "Blah, blah, blah," but his tone did.

"That's a big part of it, sure, but rethink it. Go deep. Hold up your marriage to Julie against that verse. Hold up your relationship to the Lord in light of that verse."

Ethan swirled the last of the water in his glass. "What do I win when I figure it out?"

Grandma and Grandpa grinned. "When you figure it out, you win."

"Well, guess I'd better crack this code then. Does the rest of the family know this, or am I in on a rare secret?"

"If they need to know, they know."

Grandma brought over a small dessert plate and cut Ethan a piece of cake. "Good news about Elizabeth and Kavan, isn't it?"

Being reminded of the Donovan baby stabbed his heart a little and resurrected the dark memory of his fight with Julie. "Yes, good news."

Ethan imaged how his and Julie's news would hit the family. Everyone knew their journey. In fact, the decision to try infertility medications had sparked a family debate. Should they trust medical technology or wait to see what the Lord would do? Ethan decided it was up to the Lord no matter what path they chose.

Remembering caused a gnawing pain to work over his shoulders and neck.

"Are you and Julie going to join them anytime soon?" Grandpa asked.

"You're full of questions tonight, Grandpa." Ethan turned to his grandma. "Did you take away his gossip magazine again?"

How do I get out of this one? His cell phone chirped just in time. He grinned at Grandpa as he unclipped it from his belt.

"Saved by the bell." Grandpa scooted back his chair and mumbled something about a cold glass of milk.

"Hello?"

"Eth, it's me."

"Where are you?" Ethan flipped his wrist over so he could see his watch. He remembered the Celtics game and hoped to catch it.

"At the theater. My car died."

Ethan ignored the sting of guilt and asked, "Why did you even drive your car? Doesn't Sophia have a new SUV or something?"

"Forgive me. I thought you said my car was fixed up, good as new."

He rubbed his forehead. He did say that. *Stop being a jerk, Eth, and give her a break.* "What do you want me to do?"

"Come and get us in a couple of hours?"

"Can you call me when you're ready?"

"I will. Thanks, Ethan."

"No problem, babe." Ethan pressed END, muttering about missing the game and driving across town to pick up Julie and her friend.

Grandpa rapped on the table. "Lambert's Code." He took the empty cake plate and milk glass to the sink. "Get cracking."

nine

Sunday after church, Julie called Kit Merewether. "So tell me about this quartet."

"I thought I'd hear from you." Her laughter resonated like the notes of a violin. Julie wondered if her own laugh would sound like the cello in years to come.

"Have you already started practice?"

"No, I was praying for the right cello player. The Lord led me to you."

The Lord sent Kit a cello player but neglected to send me a child? Julie banished the thought. "Monday nights are best for me."

"You met the other two at your parents' last Friday night, Cassie Ferguson and Mike Chason. I'll confirm their availability, and we'll get started. I live halfway between White Birch and Manchester. We'll practice at my place."

"Sounds fun." Julie manufactured a bit of enthusiasm. Joining the quartet kept with her resolve to move on with life, to allow the Lord to paint new colors on her heart.

While music was one of her life's treasures, she never anticipated it being a pacifier for her troubles.

After her conversation with Kit, Julie surveyed the apartment, contemplating her options. She could clean, but. . . She chuckled. *Why give Ethan a heart attack?*

Despite the lack of harmony in their relationship these days, she wasn't ready to arrange his funeral.

Standing in the middle of the living room, hands on her hips, she stared out the front window. Snow still blanketed the ground, and the forecast called for more. It was the first week of March, but spring felt light-years away.

Church had been good this morning. Pastor Marlow preached from the Gospel of John. She loved the image of

John leaning on Jesus during the Last Supper. "I want to lean on You, Lord."

But she found it hard to rest in Him, hard to trust Him with every area of her life. Especially when life was not turning out as she had planned.

She and Ethan quarreled last night after he picked her up from the movies and dropped Sophia off at home. They argued about her car, his sporting appetite, and why her jeans remained on the bathroom floor.

Julie cringed, remembering her statement to Ethan as he got in bed and turned out the light.

"It's probably a good thing we're not having kids. They might be an inconvenience to you."

"Julie, how can you say that? I hurt over this situation, too."

"Really?" *It's so hard to tell, Eth.*

Recalling the conversation made her insides clench. *How do we get out of this cycle, Lord?*

After church and a quick lunch at home, Ethan took off to watch a NASCAR race with his cousins. She thought of going over to visit Bobby's wife, Elle, but remembered she visited her parents on Sunday afternoons.

Deep in thought, Julie jumped when the phone rang. "Hello?"

"Hi, Julie, it's Elizabeth."

"How are you?" Julie sank down on the couch. She loved hearing from her cousin-in-law, though it brought such a sharp reminder. "I missed you in church this morning."

"I missed being there. But ever since we saw you and Ethan at Italian Hills, I've had the worst morning sickness."

Julie smiled. "Oh, the joy." *A joy I'll miss.*

"Talk about paying the piper." Elizabeth laughed. "Kavan almost had to take me to the ER."

"I'll pray for you."

"Oh, please do."

Julie tugged a loose thread on the hem of her sweater. "I'm sorry about the other night—"

"Don't mention it, Julie. Ethan said you were having a

bad day. Kavan's with the guys watching some car race, so I thought I'd give you a call."

Her eyes burned. "Ethan's there, too."

"How are you?"

She chewed her bottom lip. "Fine. Doing fine."

"Do you want to talk about the other night?"

Julie smiled, remembering when Elizabeth came to White Birch almost two years ago, driven and determined to go to grad school but falling in love with Kavan instead.

What was it I told her? Marriage is pleasant, safe, and wonderful. Now she's moving on, having children, living my life. "Nothing to say right now, Beth, but—" She lost control of her voice for a moment. "I'm sure we'll be talking later."

"You know my number."

Being keenly aware of Elizabeth's happiness only highlighted Julie's disappointment. Taking a deep breath, she cleared the frog from her throat and said, "I never told you congratulations."

"Thank you." Elizabeth's words bubbled. "We weren't planning on it. You know what they say. It happens when you least expect it."

That's what they say. "A child is a blessing at any time. Expected or not."

"It took awhile to get used to the idea, but now I can't imagine anything else."

Julie rode the wave of Elizabeth's jubilant emotion. "How wonderful."

"To think I wanted to be a nuclear engineer. This is way better. I mean, Julie, I'm going to be a mom. Me." Elizabeth chortled.

For a split second, Julie contemplated telling her the news but decided against it. It would only make Elizabeth feel bad.

A long pause lingered between them. *Think of something to say, Julie.*

"We should have your baby shower at Grandma Betty's." The words popped out of her mouth before her brain had time to process them.

"Oh, wouldn't that be lovely?"

"Yes, it would." Julie rested her forehead in her hand.

"You are my closest girlfriend, Julie. You're family, too, but my best friend in White Birch."

Julie straightened and inhaled slowly. "Well, then we should plan a spring shower."

Elizabeth giggled. "That's funny. A spring shower."

"A spring shower?" Julie didn't understand. *Oh, a spring shower.* "Yes, that's funny."

"Hey, Julie, I have a little pun in the oven." Elizabeth laughed heartily at her joke.

Julie laughed with her. "May you and your pun do well. Meanwhile, I'll talk to Grandma. I'm sure Elle would like to help—and Ethan's mom."

They chatted about registering for gifts and compared baby showers they loved with the ones they hated.

When Julie finally said good-bye, she let the tears flow. "Lord, will it ever *not* hurt?"

She yanked a couple of tissues from the box on the breakfast nook, feeling as if the dark cloud over her would never dissipate. *I need some sunshine in my life.*

When she stooped to toss her tissues in the trash, a brightly colored newspaper ad caught her eye. Ethan had stacked Sunday's paper by the garbage, ready for recycling.

Wiping her eyes, she picked up the folded broadsheet and read. *Why not?* She thought for another second. *Should I? Ethan would be shocked.* She glanced at the color ad again. With a pound of her palm on the countertop, she decided. *I'm taking control of my life, at least where I can. I'm going to do it.*

Snatching up the phone, she thought for another second, then dialed Sophia.

"Come pick me up." Her car sat dead in the cinema parking lot.

"Why? Where are we going?"

"You'll see."

Ethan, Kavan, Will, and Bobby found a booth at the diner.

"I'm having one of Sam's cheeseburgers," Will said without reaching for the menu. "And a sundae for dessert."

"In my dreams." Bobby opened his menu. "Elle has me on a diet."

"I'll have a salad." Ethan glanced between Will and Bobby's identical faces, then at Kavan. "Don't tell me Elizabeth has you on a diet."

Kavan shook his head. "Gentlemen, my wife is pregnant. Right now, the sight of food makes her sick. I only eat when I'm not with her."

They were empathizing with Kavan when Jarred Hansen came for their order.

"Do you believe that's our production supervisor's grandson?" Ethan motioned toward the young man.

Bobby nodded. "They grow up fast."

"Speaking of growing up fast, aren't you and Julie ready to bless us with a Lambert baby?" Will asked.

Bobby added, "We thought you'd have two or three by now."

Will stacked the menus behind the salt and pepper rack. "I can't believe you let Elizabeth and Kavan beat you to it."

Kavan scoffed. "I didn't know there was a competition, but believe me, we didn't think we'd start a family so soon."

Ethan unrolled the napkin from his fork, spoon, and knife. The table talk pinged the deep recesses of his heart and returned a sad sensation. "Guess it's not our time."

Should I tell them? He glanced at their faces, thought of Julie, and decided against it. It didn't seem fair to take the focus from Elizabeth and Kavan. Besides, they had yet to tell each set of parents.

Not ready to break the news to his mother-in-law, Ethan knew Sandy meant well, but she set too many of her hopes in Julie.

"Forget babies." Bobby grinned at Ethan and Kavan and leaned against the back of the booth. "Will, when are you going to find a nice girl, settle down, get married?"

A crimson hue colored Will's cheeks, and it wasn't from the heat of the diner.

Ethan laughed. "Give him a break, Bobby. He's got to go on a date before he can get married."

Jarred interrupted with their order.

"Thank you, my man, just in time." Will reached for his soda and took a deep sip.

When Jarred left, Ethan asked, "Didn't you have a thing for his aunt? What was her name?"

"Taylor." Bobby shot out her name like he'd been thinking the same thing.

Ethan nodded. "That's right. Taylor. What ever happened with her, Will?"

"She got a life. Which I suggest both of you do."

Laughter rippled around the table, and the conversation turned to town happenings and Lambert's Furniture.

"Tomorrow I'll have the contract for the new warehouse construction signed," Ethan told Will, stabbing a forkful of salad.

Will waved a french fry at him. "Good. We need that warehouse to get under way the first of spring. The VP of sales tells me summer is going to be busy."

Ethan looked at Bobby. "Is that so, VP of sales?"

Bobby nodded. "If we land every deal we're working, it'll be a record sales year."

"Sounds like Grandpa's business is doing well," Kavan noted.

"Grandpa never dreamed his furniture ideas would turn to this," Will said.

Talk of Grandpa reminded Ethan. "Have any of you heard of Lambert's Code?"

Bobby creased his brow, thinking. "I've heard Grandpa mention it but don't know the definition."

Kavan shrugged. "I've been around the Lambert household most of my life, and I've heard Grandpa mention 'The Code,' but that's all I know."

"Same here," Will said. "Pass the ketchup."

Ethan slid the red bottle Will's way. "He and Grandma said something about submitting to one another?"

"You got me."

"Guess it's up to me to crack the code." Ethan looked at their faces.

"Ethan Lambert, 007." Bobby said in a deep voice.

The men laughed.

"All right, leave it to me." Ethan pointed at them with his fork. Most of the time, he thought he had a great relationship with Julie. Though these days, they did seem to live life from a different game book.

But they'd been busy. She completed grad school and started teaching. He took over the production department for the family business. She started teaching private lessons. He learned golf.

Lambert's Code, he thought. *Submit to one another. Lord, show me how.*

Jarred brought Will's sundae just as Ethan's cell rang. "Hello?"

"Ethan, Steve Tripleton. I'm putting the final plans together for Costa Rica. Are you still interested?"

"Absolutely." Ethan smiled. Five days of paradise. How could he say no?

"Excellent." Steve listed the April dates and told Ethan his travel agents would book the flight. "What about your cousin?"

Ethan rapped his knuckles on the table to get Will's attention. "Do you want to go on that Costa Rica golf excursion?"

Will nodded. "I'll leave Bobby in charge of Lambert's Furniture."

"Sure, leave me holding the bag."

Ethan grinned. "Yes, Steve, Will's in."

When he hung up, Bobby and Kavan quizzed him. "You're golfing in Costa Rica? Does Julie know?"

"Not yet."

"Not yet? You just committed." Bobby shook his head.

"Don't worry, Bob. She'll be fine with it."

"Elle would be livid if I planned a trip like that without talking to her first."

Kavan slapped him a high five. "I've only been married a year, but I know better than that."

Ethan scoffed. "Please, Julie understands. Besides, she's my wife, not my mom."

"I can't imagine Julie's going to pat you on the head and say, 'Have a nice time.'" Bobby eyed Ethan as he dropped a few bills on the table. "Dinner is on me today."

Kavan laughed, clapping Ethan on the back as they slid out of the booth. "That may be the last kind thing that happens to you today."

"Come on, you guys, you're overreacting." Ethan waved at Sam and Jarred as they exited, wrestling with the twinge of conviction.

ten

Julie stood back, hands on her hips, adrenaline pumping. "Should I do it, Sophie?"

The lithe blond puckered her lips. "Yes, you deserve a new car."

"I do, don't I?" Julie walked around the two-seater sports car. It was a little expensive, but not much more than the van Ethan considered buying if they had children.

But we aren't having children. In the past three years, they'd spent the price of the car trying to conceive. *Might as well have something to show for the money we spent.*

She looked at Sophia. "Do I do it?"

"Yes. It's last year's model, you're getting a great deal, and it's an incredible car." Sophia held up her fingers as she ticked off her reasons.

Julie shrugged with excitement and walked around the car. "It's a gorgeous car, but I think our niece's Barbie car is bigger than this one."

Sophia laughed.

The salesman clapped his hands together. "We can use your old car as a down payment. I can get you in this fine car within an hour. It's a great deal. Probably won't be here tomorrow."

Julie chewed her bottom lip. She'd brought the jalopy's title. The salesman said they'd happily tow it from the theater parking lot. Should she call Ethan? But that would ruin the surprise.

She liked the car. A lot. They were both making nice salaries now, especially since Ethan took over the production manager's job at Lambert's Furniture last year. And they wouldn't be spending any more money on medical procedures. *We can manage.* With one last look inside, she asked, "This is the only one? Do you have an automatic?"

The salesman muffled a chuckle. "All of these models come standard with manual transmission. They are made to be driven."

"Oh." Julie wrinkled her nose. She preferred an automatic, but for a car like this, she thought she could get used to shifting gears.

"It's a beaut."

"Yes, it is." Julie followed the salesman to his desk on the showroom floor, determined to make this the first day of the rest of her life. *I'm going to do it.*

Sophia leaned over her shoulder when the salesman took a phone call. "Pick me up for work tomorrow."

Julie grinned up at her. "Should I do this?"

"For crying out loud, yes."

Julie thought of Ethan with his quick wit and decisive actions. If he wanted something, he got it. Now it was her turn. Besides, she'd spent money before, not this much, but they were two successful, working people. And she didn't even count the money Kit estimated she'd make playing spring and summer engagements with the quartet.

Mental note: Tell Ethan about the quartet.

In less than an hour, Julie slipped into the driver's seat and turned the key. As she gripped the wheel, power vibrated up her arms. Grinning up at Sophia, she wondered for a moment if having a baby could ever feel as sensational as this.

A sad *no* resonated in her heart.

"Don't forget to pick me up." Sophia stepped back and waved.

Julie shifted into first and let out the clutch. "See you tomorrow, I hope." The car lurched forward and stalled. She peered up at the salesman. "I can do this."

She maneuvered slowly out of the parking lot under a twilight sky and gingerly shifted out of second gear. *Oh my. . .*

At once, buckets of doubt poured over her. *Did I really do this? Was it the right thing? Ethan's going to kill me. No, I needed a new car. And this was a great deal.* She gripped the wheel as if to ward off panic.

I got tired of waiting. She hugged the curve that led to the White Birch covered bridge. Lights glowed from the house on the hill, warm and inviting.

Grandma and Grandpa Lambert's. She jerked the wheel right and into their driveway, sending a spray of gravel into the air. She prayed she wouldn't stall the car before getting to the top of the hill. When she made it, she sighed with relief and parked by the kitchen door.

"Hello?" Julie called, knocking lightly on the door as she entered.

Grandma Betty welcomed her with a hug and kiss. "Julie, come in."

Julie breathed in her fresh, ironed-cotton scent. "Hi, Grandma."

She wriggled out of her coat and mittens. For as long as she could remember, Grandma Betty was her grandma as much as she was Ethan's.

Grandpa Matt got up from his easy chair. "Pretty Julie. Come on in. It seems the Ethan Lambert household is visiting one at a time this weekend." He propped his book on the end table.

Julie fell into his embrace. "Oh, Grandpa, I think I made a big mistake." She slowly sat on the sofa.

"What's wrong?" Grandpa sat next to her.

Julie opened her mouth to speak, but emotion choked her words. Grandma came in and lowered herself onto the couch next to Julie.

"I'll go make some hot tea," Grandpa said.

"That won't help," Julie mumbled.

Suddenly tears took over. She'd kept it in too long: the pain of barrenness, the strain between her and Ethan, buying a car with a price tag that challenged her annual salary.

Grandma passed her a tissue. "Tell me what's going on."

Julie wiped her face and tucked her hair behind her ears. "It's all wrong. Everything."

"Come now, it can't be all that bad." Grandma picked up her Bible perched on the edge of the coffee table.

"It can be and it is." Julie stared at the ceiling while wiping away tears.

"Here we go." Grandpa bent over Julie's shoulder with a steaming cup of tea in a china saucer. "Since this is an emergency, I microwaved the water to get it done faster."

Light laughter broke the burden of sorrow. "You even put cream in my tea." Julie looked at Grandpa through watery eyes.

"Of course." Grandpa Matt settled in his chair adjacent to the women.

Julie cried softly. She pondered the words she should use to tell her story. *Straightforward*, she decided. *Honest*.

Setting her tea saucer on the table, she propped her forearms on her knees, a ragged tissue between her hands. "Dr. Patterson told me last week I can't have children."

Grandma held her hand tightly.

Julie cleared her throat and continued. "After all we've been through, the trying and waiting, we find out it's almost impossible."

"So that's what Casey wanted," Grandpa muttered.

Julie stood, noticing for the first time the fire crackling in the fireplace. "Dr. Patterson thought Ethan knew, but he didn't. When he found out, he came by the school, angry. We argued and my class saw us. It seems all we do is growl or snap at each other. The last three years have been hard, trying to have a baby. But the doctor's news seemed to expose something we didn't know was there. We've drifted apart and lost our way with each other."

"That kind of news is devastating, Julie. You and Ethan need time to process." Grandma flipped her Bible open to Proverbs. "Here's one of my favorite verses: 'Trust in the Lord with all your heart, and lean not on your own understanding.'"

Julie's voice quivered. "I want to trust Him. I had so much faith as a child, but now He seems so far away."

Grandpa ambled across the room and stirred the fire. "You've let your adult thinking interfere with your faith, Julie. Even an old man like me has to lean on Jesus like a child. Our heavenly Father has good plans for you and Ethan. Learn to submit to His will and trust in Him."

"I know, Grandpa. I want to trust. . . ." Julie sighed, burying her face in her hands. "There's one more thing."

"Can't be all that bad." Grandpa stirred the embers one last time before returning the fire poker to the holder.

"I bought a new car." Julie sat up straight. "A convertible sports car."

"I see." Grandma clasped her hands over her knees. "And you didn't talk to Ethan first?"

"No," Julie said, resolve replacing her sadness. "Life felt so out of control, I decided I'd do something about it. My old car broke down again, so I bought a new one."

Grandpa sat down in front of Julie, his chin jutted out. "Julie, you and Ethan have been through a lot these last few years. Like you said, focusing on starting a family took its toll on you both."

She met his gaze.

"But your marriage is about more than having children. You two need to work together, communicate, live by Lambert's Code."

Julie tossed her used tissue onto the table. "What's Lambert's Code?"

"Submitting to each another. Yielding. Considering each other's opinion and concerns."

She smirked and said halfheartedly, "Now you tell me."

"Never too late to start," Grandpa said.

"Julie, your identity in life is not in children or cars." Grandma closed her Bible but kept her finger between the pages. "It's about how much Jesus loves you. If all else fails, His love will not."

Julie winced. "I know it in my head; I'm just not confident in my heart."

Grandpa narrowed his eyes and tipped his head to one side.

"Did you get a good deal on the car?"

With a half grin, she answered, "As a matter of fact, I did."

Grandma stood. "Julie, pray and ask for understanding on what it means to submit, to yield to one another. You and Ethan should row in unison, not in opposite directions."

She was right. So why did Julie find it so hard to grasp? Why did God's voice seem so far away, so small?

Grandma took Julie's hand and pulled her off the sofa. "It's late. Go home. Talk to your husband."

"All right. Thank you."

At the bottom of the long Lambert driveway, Julie turned right toward the covered bridge instead of left toward home.

She parked the crimson car under the shadows of the old landmark. Lovers' initials were etched in the bridge's wide rafters for all time. EB LOVES LJ. TOMMY LOVES CINDY 12–7–60.

Ethan had climbed to the top and carved their initials into the dark wood ten years ago. Julie wandered the length of the bridge and stood under the spot where she thought he'd made their mark.

With the slow trickle of the river in her ears, she prayed, asking the Lord for wisdom—and a yielded heart.

eleven

Ethan sat in the dim light of the television, flicking through the channels, one after another, looking but not seeing.

The program guide channel told him it was ten thirty, and he grew more agitated with each second that ticked away.

Julie, where are you?

For the second time this month, she didn't answer her cell phone. She couldn't have gone too far with her car parked at the theater. He made a note to have it towed, again, tomorrow.

Out of desperation, he hunted down Sophia's number to see if Julie was with her. Sure enough, she'd seen Julie earlier but had no idea where she was now.

When he heard the small click of the front door, he leaped out of his seat. His emotions rumbled with anger and relief.

"Did you forget your cell phone?" He met her by the hall closet. He fired the question but kept his voice low and steady.

"It was in my purse." Julie eased the closet door shut, her movement stiff, her attitude guarded.

"Where were you? I almost called Jeff."

Julie walked past him with no more explanation. "Is he on duty tonight?" She flipped on the light over the stove and tugged open the refrigerator.

"Julie, where *were* you?" Ethan stood in front of the open refrigerator door and peered into her face.

Julie's posture stiffened. "Excuse me, I want something to eat." She shoved him aside.

The last time she acted like this, she had just found out they couldn't have children. What happened this time?

He touched her arm. "Please tell me where you were. You scare me when you disappear and don't answer your phone."

Julie faced him, her chin high. Wisps of her sleek blond

hair, freed from her ponytail, fluttered above her narrowed green eyes.

"I bought a car."

Ethan drew back. His jaw tightened as he held his tone in check. "You bought a car?"

"Yes, I got tired of driving that broken-down heap. Now you know." She brushed past him for the stairs.

Ethan went after her. "How can you buy a car without talking to me?"

"If you wanted something, you'd buy it." She kicked off her winter boots and slipped from her jeans.

"Not something that huge, Jules. Give me some credit. What did you buy?"

"A Honda S2000. They had one of last year's models on the lot. I got a good deal." She lifted her gaze for a split second to meet his, then disappeared into the bathroom and shut the door.

"A Honda S2000? Are you kidding?"

A muffled "No" came through the door.

Ethan balled his fists and took a deep breath. *Lord, help me out here. I want to understand her, but please. . .a Honda S2000?*

He slowly opened the door and propped himself against the door frame. "Julie, why?"

She faced him, wielding her toothbrush in the air. "Oh, I don't know. I can't have a baby, so how 'bout a car? I was tired of that broken-down heap." Julie snapped around to the sink and resumed brushing her teeth.

"Don't be mad at me; I'm trying to understand." Ethan stepped farther into the bathroom. "What are the monthly payments? What's the gas mileage, insurance, and maintenance? Did you make a down payment?"

He watched his wife through the mirror. "Julie?"

She rinsed and dropped her toothbrush into the holder. "They took my old car title as a down payment. Plus, I'll be playing in a quartet with Kit Merewether. That money will help cover the expenses."

"Quartet? What quartet?" Ethan sighed, his anger fading with the realization that his relationship with Julie was on shifting sand. "When will you be doing that?"

She sat on her side of the bed with her brush. "Not sure, but I told her Mondays were best for me."

"Were you going to talk to me about this?"

"Sure, but, Ethan, you're at the rec center most Mondays. What does it matter?" She brushed her thick hair with fast, strong strokes, then crawled into bed and set her alarm. "Were you going to talk to me about your next sports deal thing?"

As a matter of fact, yes. But he was too frustrated to bring up Costa Rica now. "Your clothes are still on the floor."

She sighed and climbed out of bed. She picked up her jeans and top and dropped them over the back of the rocker. She tossed her boots into the closet. "Happy?"

"Yes. Thank you. Where are the keys?"

She got back into bed. "In my purse."

"You knew you were buying a stick shift, right?"

"Yes." She held his gaze.

"You hate driving my— Never mind." Ethan took the stairs down two at a time. He grabbed his coat and fished the keys from Julie's handbag.

Outside, snow fell again. *Ah, Lord, the winter of my discontent.* His breath hung in the air like miniclouds, and sure enough, there under the amber glow of the parking lot lights sat a brand-new sports car, the convertible top buried under winter's tears.

❧

Julie listened to Ethan's quick, decisive movements as he thundered down the stairs, found her keys, and opened the hall closet.

When the front door slammed, she slipped under the covers and tried not to think of anything, anything at all.

This is not how she meant the night to go. He had a right to know where she was, but Julie had struggled with feeling defensive and irritated during the ride home. When she walked into the apartment, Ethan's tone pushed her to the edge.

Awake in the dark, she tried to put her finger on when the rocky moments became more frequent and more devastating. Their pursuit of a pregnancy strained their marriage instead of bringing them closer. She saw now that they leaned on their own hopes and not the Lord. To deal with the letdowns, they retreated into their own private worlds.

All the time, money, and emotional energy spent trying to conceive seemed to haunt them now. How stressful life became when they lived month to month, year to year, hope giving way to hopelessness, only to hope again. In the end, barrenness was the final judgment.

Julie rolled onto her side, wiping her cheeks with the edge of the pillowcase. Worse than the barrenness of her body was the growing desert between her and Ethan.

"God," Julie whispered in the dark, "I'm sorry about my attitude and that I bought the car without talking to him first—or You."

She pictured Ethan driving the new car, and a wave of guilt splashed against the sandy slope of her emotions. Wasn't she taking charge of her life? Grandpa's code came to mind. *Submit to one another. Yield.* They hadn't lived by that standard in a long time, if ever.

Restless, Julie threw back the covers and crossed the cold hardwood floor to gather her robe and slippers.

Music. She needed music. In the spare bedroom where she practiced and taught her private students, she lifted the cello from its case and rosined her bow.

She played freely, dissonant chords reflecting the sadness of her heart. *This will never do. I need to worship.*

Julie padded to the living room where her Bible sat on the end table. Back in the bedroom, she opened it to the Psalms.

With precise, well-trained movements, she used music to verbalize the words on the page. *I will lift up my eyes to the hills—from whence comes my help?*

The cello's soft melodies engaged her heart, and Julie released her burdens as God's Word saturated her soul.

Ethan searched the Internet for a weekend retreat in upper New Hampshire or Vermont. He and Julie needed an escape from work, music students, string quartets, bad doctor reports, and impulse car buying.

They needed to huddle up, talk, pray, and map out a new plan for their lives. Ethan regretted the Sundays they'd slept in, ate pancakes and bacon for breakfast, and read the paper instead of worshiping God at White Birch Community Church. Now that he needed God's strength and wisdom in his life, he realized the shallowness of his reserve.

A light knock on the office door drew his attention. "Grandpa. Come in." He stood, smiling.

Grandpa moved past his outstretched hand and embraced him. "Working hard?"

Ethan sighed. "Pretending to."

Grandpa sat in the adjacent chair. "How do you like your new car?"

Ethan rocked back in his desk chair. "You mean Julie's new car?"

Grandpa nodded once. "I saw her sporting around town in that thing. Very nice."

"Sure it's nice. It'll cost us a week of her salary every month."

It had been over a week since Julie came home with her new toy, and the atmosphere in the apartment was cordial but chilly.

Grandpa whistled. "I suppose you're keeping it."

Ethan stood and stretched, then perched on the edge of his desk. "We have to. She has no other means of transportation. Plus, with the depreciation of the car once the tires hit the streets, we'd lose money if we traded it in. It's not worth arguing over anymore."

"You figure out Lambert's Code yet?" Grandpa regarded Ethan as he asked the million-dollar question.

"Other than submit to one another?" Ethan searched his

grandfather's face for the keys to his wisdom. "I have an idea, I think."

Grandpa gave Ethan another single nod. "What's on your computer screen?" The older Lambert got up and walked around the desk.

Ethan enlarged the view with a mouse click. "Looking for a weekend away for Julie and me. I thought we could ski."

Grandpa slapped him on the back. "Good thinking."

Ethan peered up at him. "Am I on track for cracking the code?"

Grandpa rocked back on his heels. "You're on your way. But it's more than a weekend ski trip."

Ethan grinned. "Good to know."

"Dig deeper, son. By the way, Will owns a cabin up north. Why don't you ask him if you can use it?"

Ethan brightened. "I forgot about Will's cabin. That'd be nice and inexpensive."

"Don't know about nice, but certainly inexpensive. If you ask me, you have other business to take care of with Julie besides skiing."

Ethan chuckled, but he didn't need a mirror to tell him a red hue crept across his cheeks.

twelve

Julie lay in Ethan's arms, gazing at the glowing embers of the fire. The heat from the wide stone fireplace warmed her face and hands. The biggest log crackled and started to burn.

"This was a great idea, babe," she said, lifting her eyes to see his face.

He kissed the top of her head while weaving her hair through his fingers. "I imagined some place nicer, but—"

Julie snickered. "Will told you it was a hunting cabin."

"It's a dump." Ethan grinned at her.

"Come on, it has a fireplace and plenty of rustic character. What more do we need?"

Ethan drew her to him and kissed her cheek, then her lips. "All I need is right here, in my arms. Kings envy me."

"And the queens?" Julie tweaked the square end of his chin.

"Queens envy you. You're beautiful."

Julie loved the word *beautiful* coming from his lips. The word skipped across her mind and into her heart.

"Julie?"

"Hmm?" She felt so peaceful it was hard to stay awake.

"Want to talk about anything? Babies, cars?"

Julie's heart thumped. For a minute, she'd managed to forget.

"No." She sat up and drew her knees to her chin, staring at the fire. The large log burned steadily.

Ethan scooted closer to her. "I think we should."

Julie pondered the events of the past few weeks.

"How are you dealing with this new curve in our life? Really dealing."

She grinned. "Besides buying sports cars?"

He nuzzled her cheek. "Yes."

"How do you deal with a heartbreak this deep? With a dream that will never come true?"

"I wonder the same thing." Ethan rose from the pallet and ambled to the dented fridge situated in the corner of the room. "I feel disappointed and sad, not sure where to go from here."

Julie sensed his sadness. "That's how I feel." *Guilty, too.* No matter what Ethan said about them being in this together, it was her body that betrayed them.

"You never told me why you bought the car, especially *that* car." Ethan bent to look in the fridge. "Do you want something?"

"No, I'm fine."

"So why?" Ethan asked again, returning to their pallet with a soda in his hand.

Julie shrugged. "Life was changing, out of my control. I wanted to forget the past and press on to the future."

Ethan leaned against the couch cushions. "Oddly enough, Jules, that makes sense to me. I'm sorry I couldn't see it."

"I'm sorry I didn't tell you how I felt. It's hard to speak my heart sometimes." She grabbed his hand and kissed the back of it.

"I know."

"We need to tell our parents someday soon, I guess," she said with a sigh.

Ethan nodded, smoothing her fingers with his. "Your parents will take it hard."

Julie moved to lay her head on his chest. "Do you want to adopt?"

He curled his arm around her. "It's an option, but I. . .*we* have to have a heart to adopt, don't we? I don't want to adopt and say, 'Problem solved,' unless we know that's a right choice for us."

Julie tipped her head to see his face. By his tone and words, she could tell he'd pondered the situation.

"I agree," she said, almost in a whisper.

"I was so confident we'd get pregnant again. Now I realize

the miscarriage the first year of marriage—"

"We didn't even realize I was pregnant." Julie lifted her head. "Do you think if we'd known, maybe I wouldn't have lost the baby?" The idea stirred her adrenaline.

"No, I don't. What could we have done differently?"

But the notion stuck in Julie's head. "I could have eaten better or taken vitamins. I think we averaged about six hours of sleep a night that summer." More guilt surfaced and clung to her soul like seaweed on the shore.

Ethan held up his hand. "Stop. Julie, there's nothing you could have done. We didn't know."

For a few seconds, Julie relived that one hot night nine years ago when she discovered she was pregnant and losing a baby at the same time. The joy was crushed by the heartache.

"I wonder how different our lives would be if that child had lived."

"Don't go there, sweetie. We can't know. Besides, God has plans for us, right?"

"I want to believe He does." Julie scooted over to the fireplace and wedged another log on the fire. She hated to see the hot embers die.

When she returned to Ethan, he pulled her down to him.

She laughed. "You have that look in your eye, Ethan Lambert."

He kissed her, brushing her hair from her face. "What look?"

"You know what look." Julie returned Ethan's kiss and let her worries melt away in the light of the fire.

※

Ethan made a breakfast of pancakes, eggs, and bacon on a two-burner hot plate. Julie curled up in a chair to watch, amused, wrapped in a thick blanket.

"You're ready for your own cooking show, Eth."

He grabbed the handle of the griddle and let go with a yelp. "Hot!"

Julie guffawed and slapped her leg.

Ethan grimaced, puffing on his hand with quick, short breaths. "Can Your Highness get some snow for my poor hand?"

Julie hopped up and found Will's old tin bucket and filled it with snow. "Dunk your hand in this."

"Ah, that's better."

"I guess those cheap burners don't heat evenly."

Ethan gaped at her. "Ya think?"

She popped him on the arm. "Don't be smart."

When he leaned to kiss her, the bucket of snow slid off the short counter. Cold snow covered Julie's slippers.

"Watch it, Eth." She laughed and bumped into him, kicking off her slippers.

"Julie, watch out for—"

With a loud clatter, the skillets tumbled to the floor. Half-cooked eggs and pancake batter oozed across the rough-hewn wood and dripped between the cracks.

All they could do was laugh and laugh.

An hour later, after frying up what was left of the eggs and batter, they stepped outside into cold, crisp air.

Julie drew a deep breath, the bright sunlight illuminating her face. "I wish I'd brought my cello. I'd put this moment to music."

Ethan pulled on his gloves. "What would it sound like?"

Julie thought for a moment and hummed a few low, smooth notes. "Something like that."

"I like it." He motioned to where a white snowy thread snaked through the trees. "Will said this path goes down to a creek."

Julie took his hand. "Let's go see."

Snow crunched under their boots as they walked, resonating in the stillness. Contentment fortified Ethan. They needed this weekend away so they could talk without tension, without argument.

A sharp gust cut through the trees. The wind carried Julie's scent and made him think of summer flowers. She'd showered that morning in the closetlike room Will dared to call a bathroom, then dried her hair by the fire. Watching her, his heart beat with awakened love.

"I'm sorry about the car." Julie's green eyes shifted from the narrow path to him.

"Babe, it's over. I wanted to get us back on track financially before getting you out of that old heap."

"Whose financial track, Ethan?" Julie fell into him.

"Mine, I guess." He grabbed her around the waist.

"Should we sell the car?" She started the monkey walk.

Ethan fell in step with her. "No, we're upside down on the value right now. We're going to be apartment dwellers a little longer than we planned." He stepped on her toes.

"Watch it, klutz." She laughed and tried to step on his booted foot.

"Okay, Bigfoot." He skipped out of her way.

She was silent for a moment, then said, "I really thought I was taking command of my life—" Her words trailed off.

"You took command all right." Deep down, he was sort of proud of her. This side of his wife rarely surfaced, and he liked it—only he wished it didn't cost them so much.

She faced him, chin jutted out. "All right, Eth, that's it."

"What? I—"

Before he knew it, she wrapped her arms around his waist and kicked his feet out from under him. He tumbled to the snowy ground, hollering, taking her with him. Suddenly cold snow slipped down his back.

"Hey, whoa, cold, very cold." Ethan scrambled away, molding a snowball on the run. He lobbed the white bomb at Julie.

"Missed me, missed me, now you gotta kiss me." She danced a jig, making faces at him.

"Oh really? Now you've done it." Ethan charged her, determined to take her challenge.

"*Ack!* Ethan, wait." Her laughter rang out like a thousand tiny bells as she tried to run.

Ethan lassoed her with his arms and kissed her with all the emotion his heart contained.

The creek turned out to be a trickle with not much to see. Ethan took a few pictures with the digital camera he'd stored in his coat pocket. He set the timer, propped the camera on a tree stump, and ran over to where Julie posed. Looking through the snapshots, the top of his head was missing in all of them.

"Hmm, I wonder if God is trying to tell you something." Julie jabbed at him with her fingers, chuckling.

"That I'm a bad photographer?" Ethan deleted the worst of the shots. One, he thought, was worth saving. He wanted a visual memory of this day.

"No, that you're losing your head." She bumped into him, laughing.

"Funny." He bumped her back.

The sun burned high overhead as they walked back to the cabin. Inside, the fire still crackled and warmed the small cabin.

"Come here." Ethan motioned for Julie to join him at the hearth. "Grandpa's been talking to me about Lambert's Code."

"Submitting to one another?"

Ethan raised a brow. "I see he's talked to you, too."

"Yes, right after I bought the car."

"I'm not sure I understand completely, but I want to try. I guess we could communicate better, stop living so independently, consider each other, and remember being married means we each give a hundred percent, not fifty-fifty."

Julie regarded him, serious. "No more surprise championship rematches or unplanned stops by the plant?"

"No surprising me with convertibles or string quartets. Don't hide the doctor's bad news from me."

"Please, what could possibly be worse than what we already heard?" Julie brushed his brown waves with her fingers.

"Something that could take you away from me." Ethan peered into her eyes. "I couldn't bear it."

She snuggled next to him. "Me neither."

He reclined on the blanket pallet, stretching his long legs before the fire.

Julie lay down beside him. "We need to fellowship with other Christians, too."

He nodded in agreement. "I admit I've missed a few too many Sundays and am a little overly sports minded."

"A little? Ha!" Julie rested her hand on his thick chest. "Sometimes I think you love ESPN more than me."

"How can you say that? Don't you know, Julie?" Emotion choked his words.

"Know what?" She leaned against him.

"There's no one like you. No one."

"There's no one like you, Ethan."

❧

Monday evening, Julie parked Ethan's car in front of Kit Merewether's home. He laughed at her when she packed her cello and kissed him good-bye.

"Where you going with that thing?"

"Practice at Kit's."

"How are you getting there?"

Julie made a face at him. "My car."

Ethan crossed his arms, waiting. Julie grimaced when realization dawned. Her little two-seater would never do. "Ethan, may I borrow your car?" How could she buy a car that was too small for her cello?

"Certainly." His wide grin remained on his face as he gave her the keys and helped wedge the cello case into the backseat.

Kit's home glowed with low lights and candles. Trays of finger foods waited on the dining room table.

"Good evening, all." Julie embraced Cassie Ferguson and Mike Chason.

"Good evening, Julie."

The first fifteen minutes, they snacked and talked, catching up on each other's lives. Kit briefed them on her plan for the group. She wanted to play weddings, receptions, parties, and festivals.

At last Kit picked up her viola and tapped her bow lightly on her music stand. "Let's get going, shall we?"

Julie patted her cello case. "Give me a second, Kit."

The quartet played together like seasoned musicians, as if they'd played together for years. They laughed at their blunders and complimented each other's musicianship.

Toward the end of the evening, while they finished the plate of cheese and crackers, Kit announced their first engagement opportunity.

"I wanted to hear how we sounded together, but, ladies and gentleman"—she nodded at Mike—"we've been invited to play at a wedding."

"Where?"

"When?"

Kit smiled. Her youthful face concealed her age. "Florida. Three weeks from now. Julie, I think it times perfectly with spring break. You may need to take an extra day off. Is that okay?"

"Yes, that would be fine." *Florida? Away from winter winds and mountains of snow?* Julie loved the idea. She'd lift her face to the sun and squish the soggy sand between her toes.

Kit explained. "My cousin is getting married for the umpteenth time. She booked a quartet that had to back out. I mentioned our little group, and she invited us down. It's a paying engagement."

Enough said. They agreed with one voice to go. To prepare, Kit planned an extra practice every week until they left.

"Thursdays? Does that work for everyone?"

"Yes."

Driving home after discussing the trip to Florida, Julie looked forward to telling Ethan about her evening and of the Merewether Quartet's first engagement. She'd have the new car paid off in no time.

Ever since their weekend retreat, their communication was better, though they still seemed to go about their own business.

The code was not so easy to crack, they decided.

How did we let ourselves get so far out of balance? Julie wondered. But deep down, she knew the answer. They grew older and matured but forgot to bring their marriage forward with them.

Then the focus became children. So much mental and emotional energy spent on talking about children, making medical decisions—which treatments to try, which ones to avoid. Did they have the money? Should they continue when the desired results eluded them?

They sifted through all the parental and family advice, heard her parents yearn for a grandchild. But that was behind them now, at least for a while, Julie thought, turning into the apartment complex. What did God have in store for them? She unlocked the front door. "Ethan?" She lugged her cello to the spare room. "Babe?" He wasn't in the den or upstairs.

She found a note in the kitchen. *Met Will at Sam's for dessert. Love you. E*

Julie peered down into the parking lot. Sure enough, Ethan had taken her car. His ferocious bark about the new car morphed quickly to halfhearted yips. He drove the sporty machine at every opportunity.

Grinning, Julie wandered into the den to check the answering machine. A single red light flashed. She pressed PLAY.

"Ethan, Steve Tripleton. Just checking to see if you got the itinerary for Costa Rica. I had my secretary e-mail you—"

Julie pressed STOP, her heart thumping. What itinerary? Costa Rica?

Chewing her bottom lip, she pulled open the top desk drawer. *Should I look in his stuff?* With the tips of her fingers, she pulled the drawer out farther.

There, on top of the neat pile, she spotted a colorful brochure and the itinerary. She picked it up and scanned for the date. April seventeenth.

Fuming, she slammed the drawer shut.

thirteen

"Jules, I'm back." Ethan hung his coat in the closet and strolled toward the office to toss the spare S2000 keys in the desk. "Jules?"

She came downstairs with her hair wrapped in a towel and green goop on her face. Ethan snickered. "There's my beauty queen."

He maneuvered to slip his arms around her, but she stepped out of his embrace. "Ethan, do you have anything you need to tell me?" She took a bottle of water from the fridge and went to the living room.

Ethan watched her walk away. Even when she was angry, her body motion, fluid and coordinated, reminded him of a symphony. She'd have been a great athlete.

"Okay, what's up?" He reviewed the evening in his head. They had a nice dinner together before she went to quartet practice. He borrowed her car to meet Will for pie, but he didn't think she would be upset about that since she had his car. So why the cold shoulder?

She regarded him for a second, water bottle in her hand, then disappeared in the den. When she returned, she dropped his Costa Rica itinerary and the resort brochure on the kitchen counter.

He slapped his hand against his forehead. "The golf trip? That's what you're upset about?" He picked up the printed Web pages.

"Were you planning to tell me about this trip or just send me a postcard once you got down there? 'Sorry, babe, I won't be home for dinner.'"

"Funny. Of course I was going to tell you."

"When?"

He shrugged. "Soon, I guess." He really didn't have an answer. He'd forgotten about it. But the excuse sounded lame, even to him.

"Ethan, what was that speech up at the cabin? Let's communicate, submit to each other, and remember we're married. No more fifty-fifty, but a hundred percent. Here you are, going on vacation without me, your wife."

"It's not a vacation; it's a golf trip."

"Don't patronize me, Ethan."

"I'm not. Don't mother me."

"Mother you? I can't ask why you're going to Costa Rica with Steve Tripleton?"

"How did you find out?"

"He left you a message. Wanted to know if you got the itinerary." He could see her shaking. "How come you didn't tell me this last weekend?"

"I don't know." He shrugged without reason. "I was up to my eyeballs in snow. I wasn't thinking about sunny golf trips."

"Do you expect me to believe you accidentally forgot to tell your wife you were going on a five-day golf vacation to Central America?"

"No, well, yes. I did forget. And I expect you to believe your husband was going to tell you, eventually." Ethan rubbed his hand over the back of his head. He didn't expect to come home to this.

"So was that big speech just for me? You can do whatever you want, spend whatever money you want, but I can't?"

"You know that's not it, Julie." He felt on the defensive and didn't like it.

"How are you paying for this?"

"Well, savings."

"Without asking me? What about getting on track financially?" She stood in the same place, the same position she did when she brought out the trip info. She had yet to take a sip of her water. "I bought a car; you bought fun."

"Do you really want to compare price tags?" Ethan picked

up her water and downed half the bottle. "And I was going to tell you."

Hands on her hips, Julie asked, "Who are you going with? Besides Steve."

"Your dad, actually, and Will."

"You're ashamed of me." The words came out of nowhere.

Ethan regarded her, not sure he'd heard correctly. "I'm not ashamed of you. Where'd that come from?"

"There goes Miss Julie, barren and silly, buys fancy cars 'cause she won't ever have a baby. One day she'll be an old lady with a hundred cats." Julie moved from the living room into the kitchen and jerked another water from the refrigerator.

"That's ridiculous and you know it. Do you remember last weekend at all?" Ethan still smiled when pictures of their romantic escape popped into his head: cozy nights in front of the fire, the snowball fight, and trekking through the woods to see a trickle of water Will called a creek.

"Do I remember? The question is, do you remember? How is it possible that sometime during that weekend, our walks, our talks, the drive up to the cabin, it never occurred to you to tell me about the trip?"

"I get it, okay? I get it. I'm a cad, so sue me." Ethan flung his empty water bottle in the trash. "I forgot."

"Sophia was right. You are a cad."

"You talked to Sophia about this?"

"No, that's her general opinion."

"You have friends who think I'm a cad?"

"Get over yourself. You just admitted to being one." Julie unwrapped the towel from her head as she went toward the stairs. "You broke your word, Ethan." She bounded up and out of his sight.

❧

When Ethan came upstairs, Julie announced, "I'm going to Florida with Kit and the quartet."

She dropped a washcloth under warm water and hung her towel on the towel bar.

"Florida? When and what for?" Ethan stood behind her, hands on his hips.

"In three weeks. To play for her cousin's wedding." Julie wrung out the cloth and pressed it against her face.

"And there's no discussion. You're just doing it."

Wiping the green mask off her face, Julie patted her face dry with a hand towel. "Yes. Just like you and Costa Rica."

"When did you find out about this?"

"Tonight, as a matter of fact. Kit offered our services when the quartet her cousin hired canceled." Julie flipped her hair over her head and clicked on the hair dryer. *He makes me so mad. . . . Lambert's Code, indeed. I have to live up to it, but he doesn't.*

The hair dryer stopped. Julie bolted up to see Ethan with the plug in his hand.

"What are you doing?" She jerked the plug from him and stuck it back in the socket.

"I was talking to you."

She resisted the temptation to click the machine back on. With her jaw clenched, she set her brush and hair dryer down and walked into the bedroom.

"Talk." She flopped down on the bed.

"Right, like you're going to listen." Ethan stood tall, away from the bed.

Julie struggled against the tears. But her emotions, tender and weak, buckled under the stress. Would their struggle ever end? The chasm looming between them seemed irreparable. Just when things were going well, another issue surfaced, bringing past hurts with it. "You started this, Ethan."

"No, you started this with that car purchase."

"Which, I note, you don't mind driving every chance you get."

"That's not the point."

"Are you saying you scheduled the trip to Costa Rica because I bought the car?"

Ethan propped his elbow on the chest of drawers. "No. I scheduled it—" He stopped.

Julie slipped off the bed. "You scheduled it before the car?" Realization dawned. "That night at Mom and Dad's."

"I don't want you to go to Florida."

"Why not?" She stood in front of him, arms crossed.

"Because we're arguing and stressing. Stay here—work on our relationship."

"Okay, then don't go to Costa Rica." Seemed simple enough to her.

"I already put down money."

"Ah, I see. You can do what you want, but I can't."

"No, Julie. Don't put words in my mouth. I'm just saying I've already paid money."

She stared into his brown eyes for a long moment. Her bottom lip quivered, but she had a clear mind when she said, "We need a break, Ethan."

He sighed, running his hand through his dark waves. "You're right. Let's take a night together this week." He stepped toward her and gripped her hand with his hands.

"No, we need a break from each other." The words sank like heavy boulders into her heart.

He squeezed her fingers. "What do you mean?"

Clarity braced her. She knew what she had to do. "Ethan, since we've been married, all we planned for was our future children and buying an old farmhouse off Craven Hill Road. Now that we don't have that plan anymore, all we do is pick and fight with each other."

"So running off to Florida is going to solve that?"

"No, I'm not talking about just Florida. I'm going to ask Bobby and Elle if I can stay with them until I go."

"What?"

"You heard me."

"Until you go to Florida? That's three weeks away."

She weakened but kept to her decision. "Ethan, we, I, need to get away and think."

"Without me?"

"Without you."

❧

Ethan positioned his car next to the White Birch covered bridge. Flashlight in hand, he zipped up his jacket and wished he'd remembered a pair of gloves. But even fur-lined leather mitts wouldn't help against the cold he felt. No, his cold feelings came from the inside, not New Hampshire's winter night.

He strolled onto the bridge, the beam of the flashlight covering the ground in front of him. Inside the covered bridge, he ran the light along the length of the rafters, remembering the April evening he'd asked Julie to marry him and how he fell when he tried to carve their initials in the heavy crossbeams.

Why is it that I'm at odds with the woman I love more than anything?

An icy breeze cut its way under the bridge. Ethan hunched against the cold. It had been a long time since he leaned on his God for help, but he knew he had no place else to turn.

"Father, what do I do? I've really bungled things with Julie."

The image of his wife crying hit his heart as he prayed.

"How do we get out of this mess?" Ethan hung his head. The flashlight beam illuminated the ground around his feet. *Staying with Bobby and Elle. . . I need to get away and think.*

It seemed unreal. The events of the past few weeks eclipsed the years of happiness he shared with Julie. Ethan hated that.

He stayed on the bridge praying until the cold got to him. He fumbled for his keys as he hustled to the car, slipping on the bridge's edge where ice had formed.

A few minutes later, Ethan knocked on the front door of the Lamberts' home on the hill. He checked his watch and winced. Ten o'clock. *Is it too late?*

Grandma opened the door with a big smile. "Ethan, what a nice surprise. Come on in. It's cold."

"Who is it, Bet?" Grandpa made his way from the living room, book dangling from his hand. "Ethan, my boy, you're out late."

"Matt, put another log on the fire."

Ethan walked into the living room. His grandparents bustled about, moving in different directions yet seemingly synchronized. Grandpa tossed a log onto the fire, and Grandma worked in the kitchen making hot chocolate.

"Your dad and mom were over for dinner tonight," Grandpa said as he returned to his chair, slipping a bookmark into his book.

"Mom mentioned it." Ethan stood in the middle of the living room, lost.

"Are you going to stand all night?" Grandpa motioned toward the couch.

Ethan removed his coat and took a seat on the sofa.

"I'll bet you didn't come here to see what your grandma made for dinner, did you?"

Ethan grinned. "No, not really, but what did she make?"

"Her pot roast." Grandpa smacked his lips and patted his belly.

"Sorry I missed it." Normally the idea of feasting on one of Grandma's roast beef sandwiches would have Ethan dashing for the kitchen. But tonight, anxiety filled him.

For a few minutes, he and Grandpa talked Lambert's Furniture business. The new warehouse plans had been approved, and Will scheduled the groundbreaking for the spring.

"Will's doing a great job. I couldn't be more proud of you boys."

Ethan nodded, feeling more shame than pride at the moment. He could run the production department of Lambert's Furniture without a hitch—organized and efficient. But he couldn't do the same with his marriage.

"Here we are." Grandma rounded the corner with a tray of steaming mugs. "Hot chocolate and cookies."

Ethan reached for his mug, though he didn't feel like he could drink it.

"What's on your mind, Ethan?" Grandma perched on the edge of her chair.

What's not *on my mind?* "Not much."

" 'Not much' didn't bring you here at ten o'clock at night."

Ethan looked into his grandma's pretty face with her bow lips and sparkling blue eyes. He'd always wanted his daughter to have those features of Grandma Betty.

"Julie and I—" His voice broke.

Grandpa and Grandma waited patiently while he gathered his emotions. Ethan got up and paced in a circle. "I planned a golf trip to Costa Rica and didn't tell her."

Grandpa let out a whistle. "I see you still haven't figured out Lambert's Code."

Ethan regarded him. "Apparently not."

"Matt, let him finish." Grandma shushed Grandpa with a wave of her hand.

Ethan stopped in front of the fire, the weekend at Will's cabin breezing across his mind. "Then she tells me she's going to Florida with Kit Merewether's quartet. I told her I didn't want her to go, and she told me she wanted a break from me."

"What does that mean?" Grandma asked.

Ethan explained Julie's plan. "She's going to stay with Bobby and Elle until she leaves for Florida. I was so angry I came to the bridge to think and pray."

"Sit over here, Ethan." Grandma reached across and patted the sofa cushion.

Ethan obeyed.

"Your grandpa and I went through a hard time early on in our marriage. We couldn't agree on anything." Grandma chuckled, with a look in her eye that told Ethan she was viewing images from her past.

Grandpa took up the story. "We'd just moved back from Boston. I felt pretty humble over not making it at Harvard, knowing Betty worked harder than I did to make a life for us there."

Ethan settled back, listening, letting his soul exhale.

Grandma nodded. "We lived with my parents. I thought since I'd worked so diligently in Boston, I could make decisions without your grandpa's input. My father employed both of us at his mill, and I often gave directions to the workers that directly opposed Matt's."

Grandpa laughed. "We charged one customer three different prices for the same cut of lumber."

"Oh, and at home, he'd help me with the dinner dishes, telling me I didn't wash them right."

"Didn't you have Aunt Barbara by then, Grandma?"

She sipped her cocoa and nodded. "Yes, my mother watched her so I could work. We were saving money for a house."

"Then I had an idea for making a piece of furniture," Grandpa said, winking at Betty. "I took our savings and bought new tools, figuring if I could produce a table fast enough and cheap enough, we could open a side business."

"Ah, the birth of Lambert's Furniture." Ethan had heard variations of this story many, many times over the years but never tired of hearing them.

"I became pregnant with your dad and pressed your grandpa to buy our dream house," Grandma added.

"What a face-off we had the night she found out we only had a fourth of our savings left."

Grandma recounted the rest of the story. Absently, her finger traced the rim of her mug. "It's funny now, but then, land-a-mercy. I asked where all the money went, and your grandpa takes me down to my parents' basement and shows me a couple slabs of wood, some shiny equipment, and tells me this stuff is going to buy me the best house in all of White Birch."

Ethan imagined the scene they described, two strong forces like Grandpa and Grandma colliding. He shook his head and said, "Couldn't have been pretty."

"Oh no." Grandma glanced at Grandpa. "I had Barbara in my arms, but before I said another word, I walked upstairs, handed her to my mother, and told her to leave the house."

Grandpa smiled. "She came back down with an invisible rolling pin in her hand and verbally beat me with it." He raised his mug to Grandma. "I bow to the master."

"Shush, Matt. It was a horrible, horrible argument."

Serious, Ethan asked, "How'd you work it out?"

"Well, we went our separate ways and barely spoke for about a week," Grandpa answered. "I had pride issues and thought I'd conquered them, but my soul still harbored that dark sin. Finally the Lord tapped my heart and said, 'Matt, are you loving your wife?' I said, 'No, Lord, I'm not.' I dropped to my knees and begged God to lead me out of that mess."

Ethan's ears tingled. Grandpa's words echoed his own heart's cry tonight on the bridge.

"That night, reading my devotions, I came across Ephesians 5, and verse 21 jumped off the page: 'Submitting to one another.'"

A light dawned for Ethan. "Lambert's Code."

Grandma nodded. "Lambert's Code. The Lord spoke the same thing to me. I had to do some repenting and submitting of my own."

"So what do Julie and I do?" Ethan had an idea but wasn't sure where to start.

"These things take time, son. Your grandma and I knew we had to submit one to another and walk in our respective husband and wife roles. It took a few years to live it out." Grandpa's narrow gaze told Ethan he spoke to him man-to-man.

Ethan paced again, wandering the length of the grand living room. "We had this plan, you know. Get married, have children, be like you and Grandma and like my mom and dad. Then she miscarried, and we decided to go to school, get established, thinking we had plenty of time for a family."

"That's not your issue, Ethan." Grandpa cut to the chase.

Ethan faced him. "What's our issue?"

"You two started with an idyllic perspective of married life. Getting to where your grandma and I are, where your parents are, takes work. It doesn't just happen. You and Julie just wanted it to happen. You can't live separate lives. How many times have you been over here in the last six months without Julie? A dozen, I bet. She has her music. You have sports. Add to that the strain of trying to conceive while rowing toward different shores. Why are you surprised at the wedges in your relationship?"

Ethan perched on the hearth. Grandpa didn't mince his words, and finding out Ethan wasn't the husband he thought he'd be made him uncomfortable. "We thought it would be simple. We'd buy a house, have lots of kids, and be a family."

"A baby doesn't make a family. You and Julie make the family. Babies come into the family you two establish." Grandma collected Grandpa's empty mug. Ethan's mug sat on the coffee table, untouched. "And if marriage were easy, there'd be no divorce."

"I never thought of it like that—the kid thing, I mean." Ethan mulled over Grandma's words. He liked the thought of Julie and him being a family, a real family. Not two people waiting.

"Go home. Call your wife. Get Lambert's Code in motion, but give it time, Ethan. You didn't get here in a day. You're not going to get out of it in a day." Grandpa stretched and reached for his book.

As Ethan stepped into the night, the moon high overhead lit a path for him in the darkness.

fourteen

Julie picked up the phone, tired, angry, weary of the upheaval. Discovering the Costa Rica trip revealed a surprise emotion—resentment.

Please be awake, she thought as she dialed.

"Hello?" The strong yet soft voice of Elle Adams answered.

"Hi, Elle. Can I come over?"

"Certainly."

Julie scurried to change into sweats and slip on her boots. She packed her overnight bag, not sure how to break the news to Elle that she wanted to stay for a few weeks.

Driving over to the Adamses' house, Julie poured out her heart to the Lord. "I'm not sure at all if I'm doing the right thing, but I need a break, God. I'm so tired, so *resentful*. How did I not know?"

Julie pulled into the driveway and the porch light clicked on. Elle opened the front door and stepped onto the porch.

"Oh, Elle, nothing is right." Julie fell into her arms.

Elle hugged her close. "I haven't seen you this upset since that time in high school when you thought Ethan was going to break up with you."

Inside, Julie flopped onto the couch. "I'm sorry to bother you so late. I'm sure Bobby's not thrilled."

Elle waved off the comment. "This time of night is his prayer time. I haven't seen him in over an hour."

Julie dropped her head against the back of the couch. "Maybe he can pray for me."

Elle curled up next to her. "What's troubling you?"

"What's *not* troubling me?" Julie rattled off the list of issues weighing down her heart, from being barren, to the arguments with Ethan, to the realization that she was resentful. "I told him I was going to stay with you guys until I left for Florida."

Elle was silent. Julie chewed her bottom lip while studying Elle's thoughtful yet serious expression.

"You and Ethan are looking to each other and children to meet needs only God can meet."

"What do you mean?" Julie slipped out of her coat, then shifted to see Elle better.

"You've always wanted children. That was going to be some life fulfillment."

Julie nodded. They wanted children, and deep down, that desire filled a void in her heart. Growing up as an only child. . .

"Then you miscarried, so you decided to focus on school and careers."

"We thought we should be doing something instead of waiting around for the next baby. Get financially prepared."

"Right, but you still had the expectation. You expect Ethan to meet all your needs. When he doesn't, you withdraw. Even more so these past few years while you tried to get pregnant."

Julie clenched one of the throw pillows. Did Elle's assessment have merit? "What about Ethan?"

"He withdraws but does big-kid things like play basketball three nights a week."

"Or plan golf trips to Costa Rica."

Elle nodded. "And you get resentful of his actions."

"I never realized it before, but I resent his ability to accept our situation and move on, while I carry this guilt and burden of barrenness. It's not fair."

"Life is not fair. You can't blame Ethan."

"But I do." Julie sat forward, chin in her hand.

"Remember, Jesus tells us to abide in Him," Elle began. "Apart from Him, we can't do anything. Jesus is the only one who can meet your needs and heal your disappointments, Julie. No one person can satisfy like He can."

Abide in Him. She'd love to be confident in her relationship with Jesus. She imagined that submitting to one another, submitting to God's plans, and giving up resentment would come easy if she was sure of Jesus' love.

Footfalls echoed down the hallway. Bobby entered the room. "Julie, nice surprise." He bent down to give her a hug.

"Marriage troubles, Bob," Elle said.

"Will and I thought Ethan seemed preoccupied lately. This about the baby issue?"

Julie sighed. "And cars, and clothes on the floor, dishes in the sink, trips to Costa Rica."

Bobby sat in the chair adjacent to the couch. "Did he tell you about Costa Rica?"

"Only after I found the tickets."

Bobby exhaled with a whistle. "We warned him."

Hearing that Ethan ignored wise counsel recharged her resentment. "So should I go to Florida with the quartet? Take a break?"

"Pray about it, Julie," Elle advised, then explained the situation to her husband.

"Bobby, what do you think?" Julie glanced at the Lambert cousin.

"Just be sure you do it with a right heart. Let Ethan know how you feel. Don't go out of spite, Jules. Most relationships go through adjustments."

"May I stay here for a while?"

Elle looked at Bobby. Finally he said, "Call him. Don't hide from him, Julie. I won't promise how long you can stay. I don't want to make it easy for you to avoid working out your problems with Ethan."

"I understand. Thank you."

❧

Sitting at his desk, creating a project schedule to reflect recent orders, Ethan could not concentrate. Today, Julie left for Florida in a van with Kit, Cassie, and Mike.

The past few weeks she'd spent at Bobby and Elle's wore on him. They'd met and talked, but the conversation usually ended in a gridlock.

The night he came home from Grandma and Grandpa's, all ready with his Lambert's Code speech, submitting one to another, he was sure she would surrender her trip to Florida. He never thought she'd really leave for Elle and Bobby's.

Will knocked on Ethan's office door, pulling his thoughts into the present. "Are you going down to say good-bye to her?"

"I said all I'm going to say."

"Come on, Ethan." Will looked his watch. "If you go now, you can kiss her good-bye. Kit's place is only about fifteen minutes away."

"If I go now, we'll argue, and I don't want her to leave upset. We've done enough of that."

"Then don't argue with her," Will said.

Ethan met Will's gaze. "Lately it happens whether I want it to or not."

❧

Julie fiddled with her watch, hoping to see Ethan's Honda zip around the corner any second.

The last six days had gone by in a blur as she prepared to leave for Florida, arranging for a substitute teacher next Monday and Tuesday, preparing lesson plans, and driving to Kit's most evenings for practice.

"Hey, Julie, hand me your suitcase." Mike stretched his hand toward her.

Julie lugged the large leather case over to the van where Mike and Kit loaded up a small trailer. As soon as they closed the trailer doors, Julie knew Kit would clap her hands and declare, "Wagon ho!"

South. Sun. Warmth. Julie tipped her head back to see the gathering New Hampshire clouds, gray and ominous. A sharp wind blew across her face, and she knew there'd be snowfall by midday.

It was hard to imagine that behind the heavy clouds the sun blazed against a blue sky. It'd been weeks since the sun broke over White Birch.

Ethan, please come. Julie fingered her cell phone, debating whether to call him. She wanted to hear his voice but didn't want to argue.

Their curt conversation from last night echoed in her head.

"Julie," he'd told her, "we have to live by Lambert's Code."

"So you've said. But just what is that, Ethan?"

Arms akimbo, he'd answered, "Submitting to one another. Yielding what we want for the good of both of us."

"Both of us?" Julie sat on the couch in the formal living room, head in her hands. She'd struggled with resentment each time he visited.

"Both, I guess." He leaned against the pass-through to the dining room, his eyes intent on a painting that hung on the south wall.

"So how do we do that?" she'd asked.

"Don't go to Florida." He must have said that a dozen times in the last week.

She would always respond the same. "Don't go to Costa Rica."

"I've paid money, promised Steve."

"And I've made a commitment to Kit. I'm the cellist."

The vicious cycle started all over, and Julie's resentment remained. She prayed their time apart would help her see things more clearly. *Oh Lord, help us.*

Kit came around the back of the van, slipped her long, slender arm around Julie's shoulders, and brought her back into the present.

"Ready to go?" She smiled. "It's going to be fun. Maybe even remove that dark cloud hanging over your head."

Julie widened her eyes. "What dark cloud?" She thought she'd done a fair job of hiding her soul from Kit and the rest of the quartet.

"The one that's been raining on you since the day I met you." Kit placed her hand under Julie's chin. "Whatever it is, the Lord is your umbrella, my dear."

Tears smarted in her eyes, and the knot in her throat prevented her from answering.

"All right. Let's go." Kit motioned to Mike and Cassie. "Wagon ho!"

Wagon ho. Julie climbed into the van and took a seat in the back, her cell phone in hand. She autodialed Ethan's office number, and a nervous energy coursed through her as his phone rang over and over. She hated the feeling of timidity that held her. *I'm calling my husband, not my enemy.*

When his voice mail picked up, she pressed END and slipped her phone into her coat pocket.

Situated in the driver's seat, Kit glanced in the rearview mirror, smiling at Julie. "Florida, here we come."

❧

Ethan honked his car's horn. The light had turned green at least five seconds ago. He sat behind Jasper O'Donnell, whose '78 Plymouth sputtered and choked when the old man pressed on the gas.

"Come on, Jasper. I'll miss her." Ethan clenched his jaw and the wheel. Honking at the senior White Birch citizen wouldn't change the situation. It wasn't Jasper's fault Ethan waited until the eleventh hour to see Julie off.

Finally Jasper cleared the lane, and Ethan whipped around him with a left turn. A speed limit sign caught his attention. He touched the brake to slow the car, but his heart raced forward.

A ten-minute drive down I-85, followed by a right turn and a left, and Kit's house came into view. Instantly Ethan knew. He'd missed her. He drove around the corner just to make sure that the van wasn't parked on the other side. It wasn't.

Julie's car sat alone in the driveway.

Ethan parked in the street. Stepping out, he stared down the road before him, straining to catch sight of the van in the distance.

Nothing.

He unhooked his cell phone from his belt to check for missed calls. There were none. *Why didn't she call me?*

He peered down the road again, and heaviness settled over

him. "Why didn't you see her off, Ethan?" he muttered.

He wanted to be mad at his wife, but he couldn't. They were both playing this game and losing.

With a heavy sigh, he got in his car as large white snowflakes fluttered from the heavens.

❧

Back in the office, Ethan called Steve Tripleton. "How's Costa Rica looking?"

"Fine, just fine. Arrangements are all made."

Ethan picked a piece of lint from his light wool gray slacks. "Nonrefundable deposits, right?"

"That's right."

Ethan could hear the question in Steve's tone. *Are you reconsidering?*

"We're looking forward to this trip. Weather's great down there this time of year."

Ethan sighed. "I'm sure it is."

fifteen

"Dinner stop."

Julie roused from the backseat where she dozed.

"Hungry?" Kit reached through the middle seat and smoothed her hand over Julie's arm.

"Uh-huh." Julie stepped out of the van and brushed her hair with her fingers, her eyes squinting. "Where are we?" She stretched. From the chill in the air, she knew they hadn't reached the Mason-Dixon Line.

"Virginia," Kit said.

With Cassie, Julie shuffled into the restaurant, her stomach rumbling.

A day's drive away from home and she missed Ethan, already starting to see things in a different light. She felt guilty and disappointed that she'd stiff-armed him out of her life by living at Bobby and Elle's the past few weeks. Subtly they'd tried to urge her to return home and work things out, but she stubbornly resisted.

Maybe I shouldn't have taken this trip. What if I've caused a permanent rift in my marriage?

Her stomach twisted with the thought. *Lord, I shouldn't have surrendered to my resentment. I should have surrendered to You. Elle's right. I can't blame Ethan.*

Cassie nudged her. "What do you want to eat? Kit's buying."

Julie studied the value meals over the counter, hungrier than she realized. "I'll take a number three."

With a nod, Cassie completed the order. Julie grabbed some napkins, straws, and ketchup packets and found a relatively clean table.

Waiting for the others, Julie checked her cell phone for messages or missed calls. There were none.

Oh, Ethan, what are we doing? Without hesitation, she dialed home.

"Here we go." Cassie came to the table with a loaded tray. Kit and Mike followed with large sodas.

Julie pressed END. She didn't want to have her first away conversation in front of an audience. She barely knew Cassie and Mike, though Kit seemed to perceive things about Julie she didn't intend to reveal.

"Are you awake, love?" Kit asked, sitting next to her, passing her a wrapped burger.

"Getting there." The grilled food teased her senses and stirred her appetite.

Kit gave her a motherly hug, one arm around her shoulders. "These things have a way of working themselves out."

Julie bit off the end of her fry. "What things?"

Kit shrugged. "Oh, life things." She smiled at Julie before regaling the group about her cousin and the upcoming wedding.

Kit's cousin, marrying for the third time at fifty, had planned an extravaganza.

"So why'd the other quartet back out?" Julie asked.

Kit winked. "If I know Tina Marie, she backed them out to give us a chance to play. I'll bet my viola that she convinced them it was their idea to quit, too."

The quartet members laughed.

"Remind me to look out for Tina Marie," Cassie said, attitude accenting her words.

Kit waved off the woman's concern. "No need. She'll be looking out for *you*."

Finished with her burger, Julie excused herself for the ladies' room. There, she retrieved her cell and dialed home. The answering machine picked up on the fourth ring. "You've reached Ethan and Julie. We can't come to the phone. Leave a message." *Beep!*

Julie hesitated. *Do I leave a message?* Suddenly the words tumbled out.

"Hi, Ethan. It's me. We stopped for dinner, and I thought I'd call. Guess you're not home. Call me later if you want. Bye."

She hung up before she said what she really wanted to say. She hadn't uttered those three simple words in weeks: *I love you.*

Julie returned to the van where Cassie took a turn behind the wheel. Mike and Kit prattled on about a new sci-fi show airing in the fall. Julie half listened, sure Ethan knew about this show's debut.

She wanted to call him again. So in the dim lights of the highway, she dialed his cell. After several rings, his voice mail answered.

Ethan, where are you? What are you doing? She didn't leave a message this time. *He's probably at the rec center.*

"So, Julie, do you have children?" Mike suddenly turned his attention to her.

A recent college grad, the young man was in his early twenties, Julie figured, but his angular face and grandiose brown eyes made him appear younger.

Julie cleared her throat. "I wouldn't be here if I did." She faked a smile.

Mike matched her smile with a wide, toothy grin. "Guess not. One last hurrah before the kids come, eh?"

A prickly sensation traveled down her arms, and she counted her heartbeats, wanting to scream at Mike for being so nosy, but how could she? He didn't know.

"My husband and I can't have children." *I can't have children.*

At this, Kit and Cassie twisted around to see her. Mike tightened his lips and looked forward.

Kit deftly changed the subject. "Anyone want to charge their cell phones?" She held a cable over her head. "My cell is all charged."

Julie lurched forward. "Oh, me, please." She wanted to keep her phone on and charged in case Ethan called.

"Okay, Julie." Kit took her phone. After a moment, she said,

"My charger doesn't fit your phone, love. Did you bring your charger along?" Kit arched around in the passenger seat.

In the blue and red lights of the dashboard, Julie could see the concern etched on her face. "No, I didn't." *Ethan always remembered those things. Wonderful, organized Ethan.*

Moisture clouded her vision as Kit handed back her phone. *I won't cry; I won't.*

⁂

Ethan banged around in the kitchen, not sure what to do with himself. Home didn't feel like home. How many times in the past ten years had he rattled around their big apartment by himself? Hundreds. But he'd never felt alone—and lonely.

He went into the living room and upped the volume on the television; the noise of the game provided some kind of company.

Wandering back to the kitchen, he opened and closed cupboards, yanked open the refrigerator, then the freezer. Sparse. Not much in the way of eats. He found a frozen dinner on the bottom shelf and decided to nuke it.

Four minutes later, he dumped the contents of the package onto a plate, steam rising from a small pile of meat and rice. Ethan took a sniff and wrinkled his nose.

"Good eating." He dug a fork from the silverware drawer and sat on the couch.

He ate but didn't taste, mostly swirling his food around on the plate. He scraped the remains in the trash, rinsed his plate, dropped it in the dishwasher, and made himself a peanut butter and jelly sandwich. Emptying the last of the milk into his glass, Ethan returned to the living room.

He flipped through the channels and fidgeted in his chair like an antsy five-year-old.

This is ridiculous. With a sigh, he clicked off the TV.

He missed Julie. A lot. He didn't mind her evenings out or her busy schedule, because she always came home to him. Since he was eighteen, he'd never known home without her melodic presence. The weeks she stayed at Bobby and Elle's he'd missed her, too, but she was in town, just a short drive away.

Now she was hours and hours away.

He rinsed the milk glass and tucked it away in the dish-washer. He checked the time. Three hours before a reasonable bedtime.

Ethan wandered to the den and fetched a pad of paper and pen. Returning to his chair in the living room, he doodled between the thin lines, feeling melancholy, forming his thoughts and emotions into words. Time ticked away while he wrote.

Missing Julie

I cannot sleep, longing to be away
*   And wandering a forest trail I know*
On a clear night, and cool, when there is snow
*   As fine as powder, deep, and some would stay*
Balanced on all the branches as they sway
*   Against the icy breezes that would blow*
Great drifts into the valley far below
*   Where in the summertime a stream would lay*
But it is winter now, when all is still
*   Across a great expanse of starry sky*
The lonely moon rides pale into the dawn
*   And I would sit alone upon a hill*
Bundled against the night, and wonder why
I am this way whenever you are gone

Ethan read the poem aloud. "Eth, man, you miss your wife." He tossed the poem into an end table drawer and banged it shut.

He unclipped his cell phone from his belt with an idea that she might have called and just left a message. With a quick glance, he saw his phone was turned off. "Ah, I forgot to turn it on after the town council meeting. . . ." He'd gone with Will and Bobby to get approval to build their new warehouse since it butted up against city property.

Ethan powered on the phone and checked for messages. Nothing.

Restless, he wandered back to her music room. It felt empty and abandoned. He thought how accustomed he'd become to her playing. He hardly heard her anymore.

Now that she wasn't here, the silence was deafening. Wasn't he normally busier than this? He'd brought work home two or three evenings a week for over a year now. But tonight, he didn't even pack up his laptop. No games to play, no company business, no wife.

"Julie, what's happening to us?" Ethan considered the last few years, the strain and stress, the pain of waiting and wondering, the sadness of Dr. Patterson's news, her confession of resentment.

"Lord, I lean on You. Submit to You." Suddenly he sensed the Holy Spirit whisper, "Ephesians 5."

Lambert's Code. Ethan jogged upstairs for his Bible. He found it on the nightstand under a slight covering of dust. Propping against the pillows, he opened the Good Book.

After reading chapter 5 from Ephesians, he understood he didn't always encourage Julie as a husband should. He certainly didn't submit any of his decisions to her. Most of the time, he told her what he planned without consideration of her wants or needs. And as for loving her as Christ loved the church. . .

Not even close. No wonder she resents me.

"Lord, teach me. I want to walk in unity and submission with Julie. We need our lives to be submitted to You—and each other."

He didn't need another tap on his heart to know he had to honor her or his prayers would be hindered. After all, she was a coheir in the same grace of the Lord he walked in.

Meditating on this notion, he prayed for wisdom, prayed for Julie, and nearly jumped out of his skin when the house phone rang.

He answered the portable on the bedside table, his heart resounding. *Julie!* "Hello?"

"Ethan, what's up?" Will's question bounced over the line.

He grinned. "Not much. Sitting around praying. Thinking."

"Oh, man, sorry to interrupt. I'll catch you later."

"No, it's okay. I'm almost done."

"I had a taste for some of Sam's pie. You interested?"

"If you'd seen my dinner, you wouldn't even ask. I'll meet you there."

Ethan hopped off the bed, grateful for the company. He slipped on his boots and started downstairs when he remembered the diner's cold temperature. Sam walked around sweating while the patrons shivered. So unless he wanted to eat with his coat on, he'd need a pullover.

Stepping into the closet, Ethan hunted for his navy merino wool sweater, a Christmas present from his mom the year he turned sixteen. It had always been a favorite garment, but even more so in recent years. *I can still wear a sweater from my high school days. Got to be a favorite.*

"Weird." He flipped through the sweaters on the hangers, then the ones folded in his bureau drawer. The sweater was missing.

One last time, he checked the closet. Then a light dawned. *Julie.* She loved that sweater more than he did. They'd actually tossed a coin to determine who had rights to it one cold winter day.

With a warm heart, he reached for his university sweatshirt. Tonight his sweater kept Julie warm. So in some small way, so did he.

He hurried downstairs, retrieved his keys, and autodialed Julie's cell on his way out the door.

By the time he arrived at the diner, he'd left her two voice mails. Why she didn't answer her phone mystified him, and he wondered if their relationship would ever recover.

sixteen

The sun's golden hues kissed the dawning sky over the north Florida beach. Julie faced the ocean, Ethan's navy sweater guarding her from the chilly, salty air.

"Did you think Florida would be so cold at the end of March?"

Julie turned to see Kit walking toward her, barefoot and smiling. The breeze whipped her long flowered skirt around her ankles and wisps of her gray hair about her face.

"It's marvelous. Imagine being in New Hampshire right now. Cold, gray, depressing." Julie lifted her face to the morning light.

For the first time in weeks, her head felt clear. The ruins of her mind were swept away with the dawn of a new day.

"Do you miss Ethan?"

Julie faced her, noting that Kit didn't bother to cloak her question with formalities. "Yes, I do."

"What's troubling you two?" Kit linked her arm with Julie's and started walking.

"Things." Cold, soggy sand squished between Julie's toes.

"I could tell something darkened your soul from the moment I met you. Is it the having children issue?"

Staring straight ahead, Julie shared her burdens, not surprised by the older woman's insight. "Yes, we just found out about it. And we quarrel a lot, each wanting our own way. I'm resentful I can't have children and how easily he seems to move on with life." The words bounced around the walls of her soul like the crashing of the waves on the shore.

"Lars and I couldn't have children." Kit tightened her grip on Julie, stumbling a little on the uneven sand. "Of course, in those days we didn't have all the medical wonderment people have today."

"It didn't help. Just drained us and made me emotionally wacky at times."

"So what's next for you two?" Kit tugged on her arm.

Julie looked over at her. Light emanated from her hazel eyes. "You don't give up, do you?"

"The Lord's had me praying for you."

Julie blinked away her first batch of tears in over a week. "Someone had to be praying for me."

"Will you adopt?"

"We don't know. I always pictured myself with little Ethans and little Julies."

"We were going to adopt a baby. The ladies at church hosted a baby shower for me. We bought baby furniture; I knitted booties and a sweater. Lars painted the nursery, built shelves."

Julie's heart swelled with emotion at Kit's story.

"There we were, a couple of expectant parents, batting around names. Leslie if we had a daughter. John for a son, named after Lars's father. Oh, we were like a young couple in love again."

"What happened?" Suddenly Julie could feel their anticipation, waiting for a newborn to fill their arms.

"The mother went into labor, and by the time the little tike made his appearance, the girl's father refused to let her give him up. So she changed her mind."

Julie pressed her hand over her heart. "Oh, Kit."

"After that, a little piece of me died. Lars wanted to try again, but I just couldn't."

"That's how I felt the day I left the doctor's office. I even questioned why I married Ethan in the first place."

"Oh, love, don't start questioning. Marriage is for more than children. I can see God made you two for each other."

"I hope so. Lately I've begun to wonder." Julie wiped the tears from her cheeks.

"Marriage takes work. And you have to communicate about your plans and desires."

Julie laughed softly. "Lambert's Code."

"Lambert's Code?"

"It's Ethan's grandparents' code: Submit to one another."

"Sounds like a good blueprint for success, if you ask me."

They walked in quiet harmony for the next five minutes, the day breaking over them, the sun warming the frost from the air.

"Where's Lars now?" Julie ventured.

"He passed away ten years ago at the tender age of sixty. One minute, he was standing at the kitchen sink, and the next, he had collapsed on the floor. A heart attack took him instantly." A longing for her husband reverberated in her voice.

"I'm sorry, Kit. That had to be hard. I know you must miss him."

Kit nodded. "Yes, but I'm so busy with the symphony, the quartet, and my friends that if I had a husband and children, they'd accuse me of neglecting them."

"Were you ever resentful? Of not having children, I mean?" Julie asked, still searching for understanding of her own feelings.

"For a while. Being barren comes with certain harsh emotions. But God healed me. He will heal you, too, if you let Him."

"I want Him to, Kit. I do."

Kit pressed her fingers to Julie's cheeks and pushed her lips into a smile. "Your life is just beginning. God has wonderful plans for you. He's not forgotten you."

"I wish I had your confidence."

"Just one word of advice."

"Yes, please."

"If you ever are widowed and alone, don't buy a bunch of cats. Too cliché."

Julie laughed, deep and full. "My sentiments exactly."

≈

It was snowing again. Big flakes landed on the office windowsill and piled against the pane. Ethan stared out, hands in his pockets. He had work to do but didn't feel much like doing it.

Three days without his wife and he thought he'd go crazy.

They'd been apart before, like the time he went on a mission trip to Guatemala. But this separation came on the heels of discord.

He wanted to see her, hold her, kiss her, and tell her everything was going to be all right. Tell her he loved her.

Right now, life seemed to be a jumbled mess. The strain between them grew obvious to their family. Sunday, his mother pulled him aside and reminded him they were there for him if he needed to talk.

He thought about Dr. Patterson's diagnosis and how they had yet to tell their parents. *We can't put it off much longer.*

Ethan turned at the light rap outside his door.

"Bobby, come in."

Bobby perched on the edge of Ethan's desk and picked up his handgrip. "Do you have dinner plans?"

"No. I thought I'd hit the diner again."

"Elle said to ask you for dinner. She feels bad about giving Julie opposite advice from Grandpa and Grandma's."

Ethan rubbed the back of his neck. "Not really opposite, just not what I wanted."

"I suppose that's the lesson you're learning these days. Can't always get what you want."

"You're telling me." Ethan shoved his desk chair around and sat down.

"What's God saying to you in all of this?" Bobby squeezed the handgrip, making the tiny apparatus squeak.

"Get over myself. Love my wife. Submit to one another."

"You finally figured out Lambert's Code?" Bobby winked at him, grinning.

"Well, I understand it. Not sure I know exactly how to enact it."

They talked a bit more before Bobby left for a sales meeting. On the way out the door, he paused. "Elle's niece is staying with us for a few days. Just wanted you to know."

Ethan squinted at him. "Okay, Bob, thanks for the warning. Is she a shrew or something?"

"No, no, she's just going through a hard time."

"Ah, so I'll have some commiseration."

Bobby fanned his hands. "Maybe. I'll see you at the house, six o'clock."

Ethan stared after his cousin. *Lord, what is he up to?*

Nevertheless, he liked the idea of company. Not spending the evening at home alone, missing his wife. He'd found Julie's cell phone charger, so he understood why she never answered his calls. But he wanted to hear her voice, not the recorded one on her voice mail.

He paused to pray for her. Instantly the Lord's peace settled his anxious heart. Now if only this week would end and she would come home.

"Ethan," Grant Hansen called over the intercom.

Ethan pressed the TALK button. "What's up?"

"Need you down on the floor."

"I'll be right there." He'd barely stepped out the door when he heard his office phone ring. He hesitated. *Ignore it. They can leave a message.* But on the second ring, he scurried to answer.

"Ethan Lambert." *If this is a vendor, I'm going to be mad.*

"Hi, Ethan."

Ethan sank to his chair, a cacophony of emotion rising within him. "Babe, I miss you so much."

"I miss you, too," Julie said, a ripple in her words.

Ethan pressed his fingers against his eyes and breathed deeply. "How's Florida?" He hoped he sounded chipper and casual, but his voice wobbled.

"The sun shines every day." She sighed. "At least the two we've been here."

Ethan swiveled his chair around to peer out the window. Still snowing. "How are Kit and the rest of the quartet?"

"Fine. We slept the first day and went to the beach. But we've been practicing today. Kit's cousin set us up with an event for tonight. A retirement party."

"Do you have enough money?"

"I took a hundred dollars out of our account before I left.

And tonight's performance is a paying gig, so I'm actually earning money."

Ethan sighed. "Okay, good to know."

"How's everything there?"

"Everything is fine here, besides missing you." Over the phone, Ethan heard the rhythm of the shore. "I tried to call you."

"My cell battery is dead. I didn't bring the charger."

"I know. I found it in the bedroom."

"I left you a message."

"When? On my cell?"

"No, on the answering machine."

"Oh, Jules, I never check that thing."

"Well, you should."

The office intercom interrupted. "Ethan, we need you down here."

He wrenched around to answer. "Be right there, Grant."

"Do you need to go?" she asked.

"Well, in a minute. I went down to Kit's to see you off."

"You did?"

"Yes. I got there too late."

"Kit likes to leave on time."

"I wanted to say good-bye. And—"

The intercom called again. "Ethan, really, we need you down here now."

"Grant, I'm on a call."

"You have to go. I'll call you later," Julie said.

"No, it can wait."

She laughed. "That's a first."

"I'm working on it."

He sensed her hesitation. "It still bothers me that you lied to me."

"I didn't lie. I didn't tell you something."

"Same difference." Her soft voice sharpened.

"No, it's not." *Here we go, arguing again.*

The intercom clicked. "Ethan, we're going to miss production deadlines if you don't get down here."

Ethan pressed the TALK button, his lips pressed in a thin line. "What's the problem?"

"The CNC machine is down. We can't get it back online."

The words weighed on Ethan. He'd have to investigate. Last time this happened, production backed up a week.

"Listen, you have to go," Julie said. "I'll call you later."

"Julie, wait." Ethan stood. "I don't want to hang up arguing."

"Me neither."

"I love you, Julie. I do."

"I know. I love you."

seventeen

Kit, Cassie, Mike, and Julie arrived at an exclusive resort on Amelia Island a little after five, dressed in black tie and ready to regale the guests with their light classical repertoire.

"What's this gig for again?" Mike asked, tucking his violin securely under his arm. The beach breeze lifted the ends of his tux jacket.

"Big hospital executive's retirement party," Kit said.

"Then we have your cousin's rehearsal dinner and wedding for the next two nights."

Kit nodded. "After that, we head home."

Julie followed them inside, thinking of the night ahead, hearing her cello parts in her head.

Kit let Cassie and Mike go ahead and fell into step with Julie. "While praying for you and Ethan, the Lord reminded me of biblical heroines such as Sarah, Rachel, and Hannah. He heard their prayers; He hears yours, too."

Julie smiled. "Thank you." She stopped walking and faced her mentor. "I'm usually not this serious. I'm sorry we're becoming friends when my life is so difficult."

Kit pressed her hand gently on Julie's cheek. "We will be great friends. You and Ethan will take me to Paris for my seventieth birthday."

Julie laughed. "Will we now? When will that be?"

"Next year." Kit winked, and Julie suspected she would never really understand the hidden depths of Kit Merewether.

&

The Merewether Quartet wowed the doctors, nurses, accountants, and executive administrators of North Shore Hospital.

"I'd forgotten the thrill of a live performance," Julie said, sitting in the back of the van, reveling in the moment.

Mike looked at her. "It pays to play."

Julie laughed. "I'd do it for free."

Kit held up a check. "Payment for the night is right here, ladies and gentleman."

Since it was late, Kit promised to buy them all a luxurious breakfast in the morning. "I'll consolidate all the money from the trip and divide it up when we get home."

Back at their hotel, they said good night and went into their own rooms. Kit had arranged to share with Cassie, and Julie was grateful for the privacy. *Lord, thank you for Kit.*

The elation of the night waning, Julie changed from her performance clothes, remembering to hang them up. *Ethan would be proud.* She pulled her hair into a ponytail before washing her face and brushing her teeth.

Around 11:00 p.m., she curled onto her bed and opened her Bible. She read about Sarah, Rachel, and Hannah, searching for wisdom in the trials of her ancient sisters.

When she closed her Bible, Julie slumped against the pillow, praying, remembering Kit's reminder that God heard her prayers. *Oh Lord, have I made an idol of having children?*

Wanting children was honorable. God ordained. Making an idol of it was another matter altogether, and becoming resentful toward her husband was even worse.

While she didn't have a handmaid to give to Ethan like Sarah offered Abraham and Rachel offered Jacob, she had thrown a sports car into the works. Julie considered Hannah. She petitioned God for the desire of her heart. She trusted in the Father. Slipping off the bed and onto her knees, Julie surrendered to the Father. "I feel like I've been singled out, and I resent it. Yet, I've made an idol out of having children. My dream became more important than You or Ethan. Father, please forgive me."

She cried as she talked to God. Being disappointed, even devastated, is one thing, but questioning her life, her marriage spoke of a deeper issue. Out of her meditation and prayer, Julie suddenly became aware of a new truth.

Sitting back on her heels, she pressed the palm of her hand against her forehead. "I never realized. . . All my life. . . Oh wow." An invisible burden lifted, and she laughed the laughter of freedom.

Julie glanced at the clock. It was after midnight. She hesitated, then dove for the room's phone.

ᴥ

Around 10:00 p.m., Ethan unlocked the apartment, the day's mail in his hand. He hung his coat in the hall closet and checked the answering machine in the den. A single red digit blinked in the darkness. Hitting PLAY, he listened to Julie's message from three days ago.

Wandering to the kitchen, he muttered, "Julie, call me." He flipped on a light and glanced at the mail. The bank sent notice that the new car's first payment would automatically be deducted from their checking on the fifteenth.

"Let the good times begin." Ethan grabbed a bottle of water from the fridge and went to the den. He clicked on the little lamp Julie had given him for studying the first year they were married.

He smiled. In those days, she liked to go to bed early. He preferred to stay up late, studying.

Yet they wanted to be together. The little lamp was their compromise. She curled up next to him and went to sleep while he studied by the lamp's thin light.

"Lambert's Code in action, and we didn't even know it."

Dinner at Bobby and Elle's earlier in the evening came with an interesting twist. Elle's niece, seventeen-year-old Abby, was pregnant and contemplating adoption.

When Ethan realized the intent of Elle's evening, he got Bobby off to the side. "What are you thinking?"

Bobby gestured with one arm toward the kitchen where Abby was making brownies with their kids. "She's a sweet girl who made a mistake. If she finds a nice couple, she'll give the baby up for adoption. Elle and I thought—"

"Julie's in Florida after the three toughest weeks of our marriage, and you're talking to me about adoption?"

"Well, I know the timing is off, but we thought if you met her, you might talk to Julie—"

Ethan sighed and peered around Bobby at Abby. "I don't suppose I can sneak this past her like the golf trip."

Bobby shook his head with a chuckle. "Not likely."

"We talked today. It went well."

Bobby slapped his hand on Ethan's shoulder. "Elle and I've said nothing to Abby. But now that she knows you, she has a frame of reference if you decide to adopt."

Ethan grinned. "We recently adopted a car, Bob."

The older cousin chuckled. "Yeah, well, I hear you, but parenting is way more rewarding."

Ethan glanced toward the kitchen. Slender and petite, Abby barely looked pregnant. Her long blond hair reminded him of Julie, and she had the same guarded disposition. Julie would like her, he knew.

With his hands in his pockets, his body tense against the cold, Ethan stepped to the back of the porch. "I'm not sure we're ready to adopt, emotionally or financially."

"I understand, but Abby has four months left, so—"

Four months. At first, Ethan imagined he and Julie only needed a few weeks to fix their marriage problems. Now he knew they had a few months, or more.

Bringing his thoughts into the present, Ethan found the remote and clicked on the sports news. He dozed in his chair, waking long enough to channel surf, then dozed again. Around midnight, he shut off the TV and headed upstairs.

Lying awake in the dark, his mind churned with the day's events. The conversation with Julie, meeting Abby, the possibility of adoption. Were they supposed to adopt? Was that God's plan for them?

"Lord, I want Your will." He closed his eyes, slowly drifting away. The phone's shrill ring jolted him awake.

He grappled for the portable. "Hello?"

"Babe, it's me."

&

"A little late for you, isn't it?" His voice was buoyant and reminded her of white summer clouds.

Julie giggled and propped herself against the pillows. "Our concert was amazing. I'd forgotten the thrill of a live performance."

"I'm glad."

"Ethan, you've got to spend more time with Kit. She's fantastic. And, oh, guess what?"

"What?"

"We're taking her to Paris next year for her seventieth birthday."

"Oh? *We* are?"

"Well, that is, if you want to go to Paris."

"I could do Paris."

"They don't have basketball or football, but you can survive a week without them, can't you?"

He laughed. "I'll manage."

"Good. Paris it is." She twirled the phone cord with her fingers and, for the first time in a long time, felt love for her husband.

"You sound happy."

She laughed. "I am. Oh, Ethan, I never saw it before. I knew, I think, deep, deep down, you know?" Her words flew at him.

"Babe, slow down. What are you talking about?"

"Me, my parents, babies."

Ethan scratched his head. "What do you mean?"

"Ever since I can remember, Mom and Dad always wanted more children. But alas, I was their one and only. Yet every holiday, every family reunion, they commented one way or another how sad it was they never had more children."

"Go on."

"Well, then it turned into grandchildren. 'Waiting for Julie to give us grandchildren.'"

"I think I know where you're going with this."

She gushed. "Ethan, having children became my obsession, my sole reason for existence. My idol."

"Strong words, Julie. Obsession. Idol."

"But it's true. I took my eyes off the Lord and did crazy things like buying an expensive car without talking to you."

"It makes sense." He answered low, as if contemplating her conclusion.

"God's plans for me didn't matter. Your plans didn't matter. Only mine, and giving grandchildren to my parents."

"So your issue is more than just a natural desire for children; it's the burden of fulfilling your parents' desires."

Julie shouted, "Yes!" She jumped up, standing in the middle of the bed.

"How did you figure this out?"

Julie explained her Bible study of Old Testament heroines. "I started praying, and all of a sudden, I knew."

"He's faithful to us, Julie."

"For the first time, I'm okay with this, Ethan," Julie said.

"Jules, I'm sorry I've been a jerk."

"Me, too." She laughed. "I mean—"

He laughed with her. "I know what you mean."

"Just making sure."

"I'm sorry I resented you," Julie confessed.

"You resented me?"

"Well, yes. I resented the fact you seemed to move on with life while I lived with the burden of being barren."

"I'm sorry I didn't see—"

She interrupted. "I didn't see it myself until I stayed with Bobby and Elle. Ethan, I want to move on with life, too, and you."

"I love you, Julie. More than I can say."

The words washed over her, warm and cleansing. "I love you, too, Ethan."

"I'm sorry you're a thousand miles away right now."

"Me, too."

eighteen

Ethan whistled a light tune as he reviewed the production crew's schedule and approved overtime pay.

Will popped into his office. "Did you buy a canary?"

Ethan shook his head and lifted one brow at his cousin.

"What's gotten into you?"

Ethan stopped whistling and motioned outside his window. "Did you see the bulldozer in the south parking lot? The contractor brought it out this morning, ready and waiting to clear the land for the warehouse."

Will crossed his arms and leaned against the door frame. "I did."

"If we can ever get past this snow, we'll break ground by May."

"God willing," Will replied. "So tell me. Why the whistling?"

Ethan rocked back in his chair, locked his hands behind his head, and gave Will the short version of his conversation with Julie.

"Sounds like you two are breaking some ground of your own," Will said.

Ethan grinned. "Yeah, we are."

"Good for you two. Listen, I'm meeting Grandpa for lunch. Want to come?"

Ethan checked the time. Two o'clock. "As a matter of fact, yes. I'm starved."

He rode with Will to Peri's Perk. Grandpa waited for them at one of the high, round tables, his hands around a large cup of whipped-cream-topped coffee.

"Does Grandma know you drink those things?"

Grandpa winked at him. "Lambert's Code."

Ethan laughed. "So you had to tell her?"

131

"Of course."

Will and Ethan shook their heads. Grandpa was a man of his word. They loved him for it.

They ordered sandwiches, and while they waited for their names to be called, they chatted about the new warehouse and the upcoming Spring Festival.

"How's Julie?" Grandpa asked without warning.

"Matt!" Peri called.

Grandpa got up for his order.

"Ethan!"

"She's fine," Ethan told his grandpa as they picked up their sandwiches.

"Will!"

"Talk to her recently?" Grandpa eyed Ethan as he took his seat.

"As a matter of fact, last night."

"Did it go well?"

Will dropped his platter onto the table. "He's smiling, isn't he?"

For a few moments, the conversation around the table stopped while the three men bit into their sandwiches. Grandpa broke the quiet. "Are you still going to Costa Rica?"

Ethan eyed Will, then his grandpa. "I'm not sure. I mean, yes, as far as Steve is concerned, but. . ." He held his sandwich between his hands.

"Something wrong with your sandwich?" Grandpa asked.

"Um, no." Ethan took a bite. A simple phrase echoed in his mind. *"Submit to one another."*

Grandpa leaned toward him. "What's on your mind?"

Ethan reared back. "Do you have X-ray eyes?"

"Only when the Lord allows."

Will and Ethan chuckled.

"I don't know," Ethan started. "You mentioned Costa Rica, and suddenly, I felt bugged."

"What do you make of it?"

Ethan stared at a point beyond Grandpa's head. *I don't want to go to Costa Rica.* But he'd spent the money. How could he throw it away?

Grandpa patted him on the shoulder. "I think you should go to Florida. Surprise your wife."

"I'd love to, but what about Costa Rica?"

Grandpa reached for his coffee. "Still stuck on that, are you?"

Ethan fiddled with his napkin. If he showed up in Florida, Julie would be shocked. Surprised. Over-the-top happy. "Will, do you think Bobby would go to Costa Rica in my place? Buy me out?"

"Now you're thinking," Grandpa said.

"I'm a little slow sometimes, but I get there eventually." Ethan sat up straight and jutted out his chin. "Will, what do you think?"

"Can't hurt to ask. Let me call him." Will dialed his cell phone while Grandpa continued talking to Ethan.

"You've cracked Lambert's Code, son. Yielding your will for the good of your marriage."

Confidence gripped him. "I'm going to Florida."

Will clicked his flip phone shut. "Bobby's calling Elle, but it looks like he's in."

Ethan rested against the high-back chair. For the first time in weeks, his soul felt right within him. "There's only one problem: I don't know how to find her."

Grandpa pulled a slip of paper from his shirt pocket. "Here, this might help."

ぁ

Julie reclined in a beach chair, her face toward the sun. The quartet practiced in the morning, but Kit gave them the afternoon off.

"Just be ready to go to the wedding rehearsal by five," she'd said.

Like the breeze, Julie let her thoughts go wherever they willed. She smiled when a picture of Ethan blew past her mind's eye. Last night's breakthrough changed her world.

Her thoughts drifted to this morning when the quartet met

Kit's cousin for the first time. She chuckled out loud when she remembered Mike's impression.

"I feel like I just got hit by a bulldozer." Mike's oversized eyes, wider than normal, watched as Tina exited, Kit in tow.

"And when were you ever actually hit by a bulldozer?" Cassie clicked her tongue in disapproval.

"You know what I mean." Mike curled his lip.

Julie watched, amused, covering her lips with her fingers to keep from laughing. They were like brother and sister. Never mind the twenty-year gap between them.

When Kit returned to their table, she looked like she'd collided with a wind tunnel. "I forgot how bossy that woman can be." She smoothed her hair into place with her hands.

"Well, when you're getting married for the third time, I guess you want everything to be perfect," Julie had commented as she speared a piece of cantaloupe from her fruit plate.

Her thoughts returned to the present when she heard Kit call from down the beach.

"Here you are."

Julie rose to see her approach. "I thought I'd catch a little bit of sun. Otherwise, no one will believe I actually went to Florida."

Kit stopped by Julie's chair, hands on her hips, watching the waves. "What happened to you?"

"Excuse me?" Julie squinted up at her, shielding her eyes with her hand.

Kit looked down at her. "I knew the minute I saw you this morning. Your eyes. . .they have a different light in them."

Julie tried to squelch her smile but lost. "God is good, Kit."

"That He is."

"Last night I went back to my room and read about Sarah, Rachel, and Hannah."

Kit listened, the hem of her skirt snapping in the salty breeze.

"I realized some things about me that needed to change." Julie explained what happened. "I feel like I lost a hundred pounds."

"Good for you." Kit patted her shoulder.

Julie dropped her head against the top of the beach chair and drew a deep, peaceful breath. At the core of her being, she still didn't understand the Lord's purpose in her barrenness. But she was weary of chasing her will. She wanted to surrender to God's will, submit to Him. For now, if children were not a part of her life's tapestry, then so be it.

One thing she did understand in the dawn of this new day. God loved her, and His plans for her were far better than any dream she could ever conceive.

❧

Ethan caught a flight out of Boston. His dad drove him down and shook his hand good-bye when they called for his row to board.

"You're doing the right thing," Dad said, giving his hand an extra shake.

Ethan looked down to find a folded bill. "No, Dad, I can't." He handed back the money.

"A gift from your mother and me." Dad waved away the return of the money.

Ethan thanked him. "You know we can't have children, Julie and me." His candidness surprised him, but the moment felt right.

Dad jutted out his chin with a slight nod. "Yes. Grandpa told us."

"I'm sorry you didn't hear it from us. Life hasn't been very smooth lately."

"We understand."

"Now boarding all rows for flight 1210."

Ethan held up his ticket. "Guess I'd better go." He lunged at his father, wrapping him in a son's hug.

When they separated, Dad reminded him, "Your mom and I are here for you two. Let us know what you need."

"Thank you. You've always been there for us." Ethan waved good-bye and jogged down the jetway.

When the plane rolled away from the terminal, Ethan

checked the time. *Four-and-a-half-hour trip, with a plane change in Philly. . .taxi over to the island. . .find Julie. . . I'll get there just before she leaves for the wedding. Barely.*

Grandpa's little slip of information that day in Peri's contained Kit's cell number. Ethan had forgotten that Grandma and Kit had friendship roots reaching back into the '60s and their ladies' Bible study. They kept in touch even after Kit moved closer to Manchester.

"I'm thrilled to hear you are coming, Ethan," Kit told him.

"Keep it from Julie, will you?"

"Would I dare spoil such a romantic surprise?"

Ethan grinned at the notion. A romantic surprise? Julie just might faint away. "I hear we're taking you to Paris next year."

"Yes, darling. In the spring."

He liked the lilt in her voice. "I'm looking forward to it."

"As am I."

Sitting on the runway, waiting to take off, he shifted in his seat, rubbed his hands together, and peered out the plane's oval window. *Surprising Julie. . .this ought to be fun.*

Ethan whispered a prayer. "Let this be the first step to a deeper, more mature marriage."

"Ladies and gentlemen, we are experiencing a small technical difficulty," the captain's voice reported from the cockpit. "We're returning to the gate to let the mechanics check it out. We apologize for any inconvenience. We'll get it fixed as soon as possible."

Ethan moaned and snapped up his cell phone to dial Kit. This was not the romantic surprise he had in mind.

nineteen

"Is this seat taken?"

Julie lifted her eyes to see a handsome man, dressed in black tie, bending over the chair opposite her. For a brief moment, he took her breath away. "Um, no."

With his flawless smile fixed on her, he extended his hand. "Alexander Crawford."

Julie hesitated but took his hand. "Julie Lambert."

"Nice to meet you." His eyes were the bluest she'd ever seen, and his features were perfect and even as if sculptured by a master.

She tugged her hand away from his. *Where's the rest of the quartet?* They'd taken a break midreception for the cake cutting and bouquet toss. With cake and punch in hand, Julie picked an empty table in the back of the room. Mike and Cassie promised to join her, but she had yet to see them. Kit, she knew, was visiting with the family.

"How long has the Merewether Quartet been together?" Alexander asked, tipping his head to one side. His question did not reflect the expression on his face.

Julie held her hands in her lap as if to shrink away from him. "About a month."

His brow rose. "Really? You're quite polished."

"We've worked hard." His presence made her skin prickle.

"I'm having a little get-together at my home on the beach tomorrow night. I know it's late notice, but—"

Oh, that's it. Julie exhaled. "You need to ask that lady over there. She's the boss." She pointed across the room to Kit.

He followed the line and frowned. "Maybe you could come if the quartet is busy." He scooted his chair closer to hers.

She laughed. "I'm only prepared to play with the quartet."

She fiddled with her fork and plate, pressing leftover cake icing into miniature pancakes. She didn't like the way he watched her.

"Forget the cello. What about you and me?" His tone said way more than those simple words. "You're a beautiful woman, Julie." He leaned forward and slithered his fingers across her arm.

His touch burned. She rocketed to her feet, fear creeping down her spine. "I'm married, Mr. Crawford."

He shrugged and pulled on her arm so she sat down again. "I'm not." He moved closer. "Is your husband here?"

"No, he's in New Hampshire." She regretted the words as soon as they left her mouth.

"Good for me then." He inched his chair toward her again.

Julie tried to push back her chair, but one of the legs was tangled with another chair. His warm, sticky breath made her nauseous. He'd been drinking. His smile, which first appeared flawless, now appeared evil.

Where does he get the right? She looked directly into his eyes. "Please leave."

"Only if you come with me?" He sat so close his leg touched hers.

She rose to her feet. "Excuse me." As she walked away, Alexander Crawford's sardonic laugh followed.

Oh Lord, oh Lord, help. Julie found Kit with her mother and aunt. She waited for a break in their conversation before whispering, "I need to see you."

Kit finished up and walked with Julie to the outside deck. The horizon, dark and ominous, harbored the sounds of the surf.

Kit propped her arms on the railing and lifted her face to the wind. "Hard to imagine being alone at sea when it's so dark, isn't it?"

The lump in Julie's throat kept her from speaking. "Mm-hmm," she muttered. She shivered and rubbed her arms with her hands.

Kit faced her. "What's troubling you?"

"I want to go home." Her teeth chattered, but she bit her lower lip to keep it from quivering.

"Now?"

"I don't belong here, Kit. I belong at home with Ethan, working on our marriage." She batted away tears. If she cried, her mascara would smudge, and they had another set to play before the evening ended.

Kit smiled and drew her into a hug. "We leave in a few days; can you wait?"

"A man came on to me in there." Julie wrenched her arm around, motioning to some obscure point behind her. "He mocked me when I told him I was married."

"A guest?"

Julie shivered. "Yes, a guest." She squeezed her eyes shut. "Kit, he was evil."

Kit put her arms around her. "I'm sorry, Julie. Tina Marie and Marco have unusual friends."

"Unusual?" Julie shook in the cold. "I've always known Ethan was special, but this week, I've realized how special. He is an amazing man, flaws and all."

"Being apart awakens love, doesn't it?"

"Too bad it took a personal crisis and one slimeball to make me realize it."

"Here, let me pray for you." Kit put her hand on Julie's back and asked the Lord for peace and protection.

Julie wiped the tears from her face as Kit said amen. "How much time do I have before the next set?"

Kit held up her watch, catching light from the reception hall. "Ten minutes. She's about to toss the bouquet."

"I want to freshen up in the ladies' room."

Julie found her purse shoved into a corner by the bandstand. She dusted it off and thanked the Lord for His peace. Kit motioned for her to hurry, so Julie darted down a long hall toward the door marked LADIES.

She stopped short when Alexander Crawford came into

view. "I knew you'd come down this hall sooner or later."

ᴓ

The plane touched down with a bounce and slowed with such force that Ethan lurched forward. But he didn't care. He was on Florida soil.

Eight o'clock. The delay in Boston caused him to miss his connection in Philadelphia. They shuffled him over to another flight that was full, then listed him on standby for a third flight.

He got the last seat on that flight, but they sat on the runway for thirty minutes. Still, the journey stirred a yearning in him. He couldn't wait to see Julie.

Once he deplaned, he ran through the terminal, his garment bag slung over his shoulder, anticipation mingling with adrenaline. Hailing a taxi, he climbed in the back and told the driver the reception hall address.

Amelia Island seemed like light-years from the airport. "Here you go." The cab driver glanced over his shoulder. "That'll be twenty-six eighty-nine."

Ethan dropped a couple of twenties over the seat. "Keep the change."

Standing outside the Plantation Resort, he ignored his rapid heartbeat and headed inside just as the bride tossed her bouquet. A gaggle of single ladies vied for the prize. Ethan couldn't suppress his smile when a lanky, pink-clad bridesmaid nearly toppled a flower girl to catch the cluster of roses.

Roses. Ah, he meant to buy Julie a rose at the airport but in his haste forgot. He spied a bouquet of carnations on an empty reception table and asked a passing waiter if he could take one.

"Help yourself."

Ethan selected one white carnation for Julie and surveyed the candlelit room. *Where are you, babe?*

"Ethan, darling, you've arrived. I was worried." Kit floated his way, dressed in a black evening gown, her arms extended.

"Finally." Ethan returned her hug, the edge of his nerves softening. "Where's Julie?"

Kit winked. "She's gone to powder her nose." She pointed across the room toward a narrow hall. "Why don't you go wait for her? When she comes out. . . Oh, a white carnation. Won't she be surprised."

Ethan gripped Kit's elbow lightly. "Will she?"

"How can you ask? Yes, more than you know. More than you know." She patted his cheek, then took his garment bag. "I'll set this with our things."

Walking between the tables, adorned with linen cloths and golden hurricane lamps, Ethan dug his hands in his jeans pockets. He'd planned to change into a suit, but that was before the delay.

Entering the hallway, he heard voices. "Let me go."

"Oh, come on. You and me." An eerie laugh reverberated off the block walls.

"I said, let me go."

Ethan squinted in the dim light. Through the shadows he saw a large man pressed against. . .Julie!

❧

If this was terror, Julie never wanted to taste it again. She shook so hard she could barely catch her breath. "I don't understand what you want with me." She thought to run but couldn't command her feet.

"What does any man want with a beautiful woman?" He sauntered her way, hands in his tuxedo pants pockets, his shirt collar open, his bow tie dangling around his neck.

Jesus, rescue me. Julie's heart whispered prayers her lips could not utter. She felt frozen by Alexander Crawford's visual embrace.

Well, she would not be prey. "Step away."

He reached for her, but she fumbled backward, out of his grasp. "What, you don't want a little Florida fling?"

"Absolutely not!" She tightened her jaw. "Let me go."

The hallway reverberated with his low laugh. "Perhaps the lady protests too much?"

"I said, let me go!"

Julie heard footfalls at the other end of the hall. "You heard her; let her go." With long, purposeful strides, she watched Ethan travel the long hallway.

She ran to him. "Ethan! What are you doing here?" She couldn't stop trembling.

Ethan wrapped her in his arms, smoothed her hair with his right hand, and cradled her head on his shoulder. His left hand encircled her waist. "Shh, babe, it's going to be all right."

"He. . .followed. . .me." Her words came between wobbly sobs.

"He's gone now. I'm here."

She locked her arms around him as if to crawl inside his skin. With an easy sway, Ethan rocked her from side to side until she'd cried every tear. Finally, she drew a deep, steadying breath. Ethan's fragrance, musty like the scent of the beach at the end of the day, filled her senses.

She wondered if she could love him any more than she did at this very moment. At last, she lifted her face to his. "I'm never leaving home without you again."

He laughed, then lowered his lips to hers. "Never?" he asked after their first kiss in weeks.

"Never." She tiptoed to kiss him again. He tasted sweet.

"For you." He handed her a white carnation. "I wanted it to be a rose, but. . .long story. I'll tell you later."

She took the flower and kissed him again. "Any flower from you is as precious as a rose. Thank you."

Kit appeared around the corner. "Hurry, Julie. Two minutes."

"Oh, Kit, my face."

Ethan kissed her forehead. "It's beautiful."

"No, it's not. Let me touch up my makeup." Julie handed him her carnation and dashed for the ladies' room. Her hands trembled slightly as she touched up her foundation and eye makeup.

Ethan stood guard outside the door. When she emerged, he slipped his arm around her waist as they walked toward the bandstand. "Who was that man?"

"Some man named Alex Crawford. He approached me when I was sitting alone, eating cake."

"Alex Crawford. The football player?" Ethan glanced around the room.

"I don't know about football, but he's a first-class stalker."

"Is he still here?"

Julie set her carnation and purse by the bandstand. Mike and Cassie had already taken their seats. "Don't tell me you want his autograph, Ethan."

He held her close. "Autograph? I want to ask him to step outside to discuss his rude behavior."

"No fighting, Ethan." Sixty seconds with Alexander Crawford terrified her, but she didn't want Ethan drawing attention to the situation by confronting him. She felt a deep compassion for women who had no one to rescue them from the Alexander Crawfords of the world.

But she had Ethan. Suddenly he was there to rescue her. "Ethan."

He stopped scanning the room and gazed down at her. "Yeah, babe."

"What are you doing here?"

"Chasing my wife to the ends of the earth to let her know how much I love her and how important she is to me."

Julie smiled. "Did your grandpa give you that line?"

He chuckled. "No, but he did teach me about Lambert's Code."

"We both have a lot to learn about Lambert's Code." She laced her fingers through his. "I'm glad you're here."

"I'm not going to Costa Rica."

She stiffened. "Really?"

"Not if it means driving a deeper wedge between us."

"But I put a wedge between us. I came here when you asked me not to, and I bought a car without your knowledge."

He kissed her hand. "We both made mistakes. I'm here because I want to start new. We're not teenaged newlyweds anymore, Julie, playing house with dreams of babies."

"It's real life—with hard decisions." Tears dropped from the edges of her cheeks.

He wiped them away. "With disappointments. We can't let every unexpected turn challenge our love and commitment."

She pulled him toward her and kissed him. "I'm sorry about everything. Forgive me?"

"Absolutely. Forgive me?"

"Yes." She sealed her promise with another kiss.

"It's behind us."

Kit floated toward the bandstand, waving a piece of paper.

"Tina had the presence of mind to pay me." Kit flashed the check for the group to see.

Ethan whistled low. "Where do I sign up?"

Julie laughed. "You can't play a note." She stepped onto the bandstand, still marveling at the dramatic events of the evening and the miracle of her rescue by Ethan.

twenty

From the kitchen, Julie called up to Ethan, "There's nothing to eat!"

"Peanut butter and jelly."

She laughed. "Didn't you shop while I was gone?"

"Naw, what for?" He descended the stairs two at a time.

Walking into the kitchen, Ethan thanked God for His mercy and the lesson of Lambert's Code. He'd never forget it.

"I feel like pizza," he said, hugging Julie. The day and a half they'd spent in Florida revived their relationship.

"You want to go out?" She wrapped her arms around him and kissed him.

"No, let's order in." He kissed her cheek. "I'll build a fire in the fireplace."

Julie gave him a quick squeeze before letting go. "I'll call Giuseppe."

❧

The fire crackled as they dove into the large pepperoni pie. Julie twisted the cap off a two-liter bottle of diet soda and poured.

"Bobby and Elle introduced me to someone the other night," Ethan said, bringing up Abby for the first time.

Julie paused from pouring to look at him. "Introduced you to someone?" She tipped her head.

He took a bite of his pizza. "Yeah, a woman." He couldn't hide his grin.

"What?" She set down the soda bottle. "Ethan, don't mess with me. I'm fragile."

He coughed. "Please. You're a rock."

"What woman?"

"Elle's niece, Abby."

Julie tore a slice of pizza off for herself. "I met her once. She was the prettiest ten-year-old I'd ever seen."

"She's seventeen now. And pregnant."

She swallowed her pizza with one gulp. "You're kidding."

"If she finds a family she likes, she'll give the baby up for adoption." Ethan studied her expression.

"When is she due?"

"About four months. Bobby and Elle asked us to consider adopting the baby."

"You didn't say anything to Abby, did you?"

Ethan held up his hand. "Not on your life. I learned my lesson."

Julie arched over the pizza box to give him a kiss. Wiping her hands with a napkin, she asked, "What do you want to do?"

Ethan shrugged, his emotions rising to the surface. "When I pictured children, they were ours. A daughter who could dunk a basketball while humming Beethoven, and a son who loved the arts as much as he loved scoring touchdowns."

Julie nodded. "And children who love the Lord with all their heart, mind, soul, and strength?"

He regarded her, his gaze intent on her oval face. "Yes. In fact, I'd like to work on that aspect of my own life."

"Me, too." Moving the pizza box, Julie sat cross-legged in front of her husband. "You know, almost every girl wants to be a mom."

Ethan nodded and took her hand in his.

"But trying to bear my parents' load made my desire more intense."

"Right."

"For the first time in years, I feel like I have choices. I'm pretty sure it will include adoption, but not right now. God has something for me to do; I just need to discover what. Is that all right?"

He pressed her hand against his chest. "Yes, that's all right. I want to discover God's plan for us as much as you do."

"Well, hold on to your hat—"

"I don't have a hat." He chuckled low and pulled her to him.

"Ha-ha. Ethan, we're on an adventure. . . ."

He nuzzled her neck. "Mm-hmm."

She responded to his tenderness with a kiss, then asked, "Are you paying any attention to me at all?"

He cleared his throat. "Yes, adventure." He brushed a strand of hair away from her face.

"I feel released, Ethan. Like I can stop trying to fit my life into this perfect picture box."

"I know what you mean. I feel like I can stop holding my breath." He picked up another piece of pizza.

"When it's quiet in my soul, I stop thinking how unfair all this is, and you know what I want the most?"

"What?"

"To be with you. Just you and me in a new adventure with the Lord."

"Me, too. So what about Abby?"

Julie's eyes glistened. "I want to wait." She laughed softly. "I can't believe I just heard myself say that, but it's all my heart can do at the moment."

"Actually, I feel the same way." Ethan stared at her for an intense second, then closed the pizza box and said, "Put on your coat; we're going for a ride."

❧

The moon reminded Julie of a rare pearl set against black velvet with diamonds scattered around. The celestial body's white halo lit the winter sky, and moonbeams danced over the tiny town of White Birch.

Ethan escorted her to the convertible, blankets tucked under his arm.

"Where are we going?" She waited by her door, shivering.

"It's a surprise." Ethan opened her door, then reached inside to pop the top.

Julie took the blankets he handed her, laughing. "What are you doing? It's freezing."

With the top tucked away, Ethan motioned to the passenger

seat. "Your chariot awaits."

Enjoying the impromptu moment, Julie dropped into her seat with a giggle. Ethan spread the blankets over her legs and lap. Last, he plopped a wool beanie on her head.

Content and happy, Julie situated the beanie on her head while Ethan scooted around to the driver's side. He started the engine, cranked the heater, and tuned the radio station to something soft.

Shifting into gear, he tapped on the dash. "It's a modern sleigh ride. We've got two hundred and forty horses."

Julie dropped her head against the seat rest and sang, "Just hear those sleigh bells jingling—"

Ethan joined the song as he took the back roads across town.

"You still haven't told me where we are going," Julie said, her eyes on the night sky.

"You'll see."

In a moment or two, she knew, when the old bridge came into view.

"Perfect," she whispered as Ethan escorted her down the riverbank in the light of the moon.

The night was beautiful and serene, and the lullaby of the river serenaded them. With their arms around each other, they stood on the bank without speaking. For the first time in a very long time, Julie felt like she was running on the right track.

"Come to the bridge." Ethan guided her to the cover of the town landmark. He pulled a flashlight from his pocket and clicked on the small lamp.

"What's wrong? You look so serious." Julie lightly touched his cheek.

Ethan grinned and stuck the flashlight under his chin. "How 'bout now?"

She laughed and batted the light away. "Scary."

Ethan wrapped her in his arms. "My beautiful wife." He bent down on one knee.

"What are you doing?" She dropped to her knees, too, and faced him.

Eye to eye, Ethan said, "Julie, I asked you to marry me almost eleven years ago. We were barely eighteen, young and immature, but in love."

She let out a nervous giggle. "Ethan—"

"Shh, just listen. A lot of things have changed since I asked you to marry me."

"Yes," she said with an easy shake of her head.

Ethan grabbed her hands. "But life has taken a different turn. We have a new tapestry to create for our marriage. So"—he paused for a kiss—"with that in mind, Julie Hanover Lambert, will you be my wife? No expectations except to love and serve each other, and love God with our whole hearts?"

She smiled, her head cocked to one side. "I am your wife, now and forever."

Ethan looked at her, drawing a deep breath. "We've spent the past ten years trying to execute the life we thought we wanted at sixteen. Now, here we are adults, mature—"

Her laugh billowed around him. "Don't throw that word around too loosely, bud. Mature?" She pressed the tip of her nose to his.

He chuckled. "Given, I have my moments. But we know more what I'm about, what you're about, what curveballs life has pitched to us."

"We know the melody of our song."

"We know the rules of the game."

Tears slipped down her cold cheeks. "The last few weeks seem like a nightmare. I don't want to ever do that again."

He brushed away her tears with the tips of his fingers. "So tonight let's declare a fresh start. You and me. We might adopt ten kids, or move to Florida, maybe live to be a hundred and die side by side, holding hands. The possibilities are endless."

Throwing her arms around him, she shouted to the rafters. "And, I'll be your wife. For the next decade and every decade after."

With a hoot, Ethan hopped to his feet and whipped out his pocketknife. "I carved our initials the first time I asked you. Guess a second proposal deserves a second carving."

"Don't fall this time." Julie laughed as she watched her husband scale the side of the bridge and, hanging from the rafters, carve their initials into the strong bridge beam.

Monday morning, Ethan tossed his sports bag in the foyer by the front door. The aroma of coffee filled the apartment. Walking into the kitchen, he kissed his wife.

"Mom called. She wants us to come to dinner tomorrow night. Is that okay?" Julie handed him a plate of eggs and toast. She smoothed his cheek with the palm of her hand.

"Fine with me. I was thinking of playing some hoops after work tonight. Is that okay with you?"

They stared at each other for a second, then laughed in unison. Ethan held up his hands. "Are we taking this code thing too far?"

Julie sat down at the nook with him. "Well, maybe just a little. Besides, we have dinner with Elizabeth and Kavan tonight."

"Oh, right. I'll play another night." He bit into his egg. "I suppose we'd better break the news to your mom and dad tomorrow."

Julie reached for the butter. "We should have told them this weekend when we had lunch with them after church."

"You're right. I just know it will hit your mom hard." He sipped his coffee.

Julie nodded, spreading a thin layer of butter on her toast. "It will, but she's a strong woman. If we wait too long, they'll hear it from someone else, and that's not right. They need to hear it from us."

"Do you know why they never adopted?"

"Dad didn't have the inclination. At least that's what sticks out in my mind."

Ethan finished his breakfast and took his plate to the

kitchen sink. He checked his watch. "It's getting late. We'd better hurry."

One last bite and Julie finished her breakfast. She passed her plate to Ethan, who stood by the dishwasher waiting, and said with a wink, "One of these days, I'm going to learn how to use that thing."

"Warn me first so I don't have a heart attack."

"Ha-ha, what a funny man for a Monday morning."

In a few minutes, Ethan met her at the door. "Should we meet here before going over to Elizabeth and Kavan's? I might just go over from work."

She tiptoed to kiss him. "Okay, be there by six."

Outside, a chilly breeze cut through the parking lot. Ethan stopped Julie before she went to her car. "I want to pray for you before you go. I liked what Pastor Marlow said in church yesterday about speaking blessings over our families."

"I'd love a blessing." Julie leaned her head against his chest.

Ethan set his laptop down and encircled her with his arms. "Bless my wife, Lord, my good wife. I pray she would know how much You, and I, love her."

Julie looked up at him with moist eyes when he said amen. "Thank you, Ethan. I pray the same for you."

Ethan watched Julie drive away, wincing as the car jerked and sputtered out of the apartment complex. He made a mental note to work with her on shifting gears in a high-performance car. Her old jalopy drove like a tired mare compared to the horsepower of the S2000.

When the car vanished from his view, he walked toward his car and called his grandpa. "Can you meet downtown at three o'clock?"

"I'll be there."

twenty-one

The first week of April, Julie swerved into the school parking lot with zeal for the day—and an idea.

Walking through the front doors as the first bell rang, she dug her cell phone from her purse and dialed Grandma Lambert.

"Hi, Grandma." Julie walked the hall with dozens of kids scurrying to class.

"Julie, good morning. What can I do for you at this hour?"

"I need help planning a surprise."

"I'm your woman." Grandma suddenly sounded ten years younger. "Who are we surprising?"

"Ethan." Julie entered her classroom as the second bell tolled. "The night we got back from Florida, we took a ride to the bridge and Ethan asked me to marry me again."

Grandma chuckled. "I see. Florida must have gone well."

Julie smiled. "Yes, it did." She motioned for her class to come in and settle down.

"Good for you! So what do you have in mind?"

"Well, it occurred to me that when a man asks a woman to marry him, a wedding should follow."

Grandma caught her breath. "A second wedding."

"Well, there *was* a second proposal."

"A grand idea, my dear."

Sophia popped into the classroom as Julie made final arrangements to meet Grandma at Peri's Perk after school.

"How was your weekend?" Sophia whispered as Julie pressed the END button on her cell.

"Wonderful."

Sophia cocked her head to one side. "So I see. You're glowing. By the way, you never told me about Florida."

"I'll talk to you about it later." Julie tapped her watch.

Sophia left after making Julie promise to have lunch with her and give her all the details.

Julie's thoughts were all over the place when she finally called her first class of the day to order. Where to have the ceremony? When? How to get Ethan there? Would she get any teaching done today? She was too excited to focus. Until Miles Stanford raised his hand.

"What are we playing for the spring recital, Mrs. Lambert?"

"You mean you haven't been practicing? Oh, Miles." With a chuckle, Julie went to the blackboard and scribbled out the recital program, again.

❧

Ethan waited outside Earth-n-Treasures, slumping down in the driver's seat, hoping no one would see him. When Grandpa tapped on his window, he jerked forward.

"Why are you ducking down like a teenager skipping school?" Grandpa asked as Ethan stepped into the street.

"I don't want any of Julie's friends to see me."

"Well, let's get going then."

A red velvet strip with silver bells rang out when Ethan pushed open Earth-n-Treasures' front door. Some of the letters on the glass had been scraped away with the swishing of the bells back and forth.

Cindy Mae, the store's owner, came around the counter to greet him. "How's my favorite Lambert?"

Ethan gave her a slight hug. "I bet you say that to all the Lamberts."

"I was talking to your grandpa." Cindy Mae tossed her thick blond braid over her shoulder with a sly grin and hugged the Lambert patriarch.

Grandpa chuckled. "How are you, Cindy Mae?"

"Meaner than a bear in winter."

Ethan laughed. "Spring's around the corner, Cindy Mae." He leaned over the jewelry case.

Cindy Mae walked around. "What can I help you gentlemen with today?"

"Something for Julie. A ring. Not expensive, but not cheap. I can't spend too much right now." Ethan pointed over his shoulder at his grandpa. "I brought him along to help me choose."

Cindy Mae pulled a few items out of the case. "I saw her driving around in a fancy sports car."

"Right." Ethan focused on the pieces Cindy Mae passed under his gaze, not willing to rehash the car ordeal with her. He loved her like a neighbor, but she was one of the strongest links in the town's gossip chain.

"Are you looking for an anniversary band, a new diamond, what?" Cindy Mae placed several more pieces in front of him.

Ethan examined each one, soliciting Grandpa's opinion. They were all pretty but too ordinary. He wanted something unique and extraordinary, like Julie.

After fifteen minutes of telling Cindy Mae no and asking to see something else, she said, "I suppose I could design you a piece."

He hesitated. "Well—"

"Oh, wait." Cindy Mae clapped her hands. She dashed into a back room, hollering over her shoulder, "Brill and I just returned from an estate sale."

With a grimace, Ethan confessed to Grandpa, "A few months from now, I could afford this better, but since I asked her to marry me again, I was hoping—"

"Let's wait and see what Cindy Mae brings out. You never know, son. The Lord just might surprise you." Grandpa rocked back and forth on his heels, hands in his pockets.

"Here we go." Cindy Mae emerged from the back room. She set a cardboard box on the counter with a thump. Dust billowed.

Ethan's heart wilted. *What in the world could be in that box for Julie—a Cracker Jack prize?*

He couldn't look. Instead, he let Grandpa peer into the junk box while he studied more rings under the glass counter.

I have about two grand to spend. Maybe if I talk to Will

about next quarter's bonus. . . He sighed. They really needed to concentrate on paying off the last of their medical bills and replenishing their savings. He didn't want to live in that apartment forever. What if they decided to adopt? Should they start saving for that right now?

Besides all that, he felt a little guilty spending the money without consulting Julie. But surely surprises didn't fall under Lambert's Code, did they?

"Ah, here it is." Cindy Mae's voice echoed across the small shop as she pulled out a velvet ring box. She popped open the lid and showed it to Grandpa.

Ethan leaned on the counter and watched his grandpa's expression. One snarl and he'd know. But the older man smiled. Big.

"I think we've found a winner."

Ethan hurried over. He saw a dingy band with delicate vines winding between two diamond and two emerald stones. *What? It's hideous.* He didn't know what to say, so he asked, "How much?"

Cindy Mae twisted up her face like she was about to announce he'd won a million dollars. "How much do you want to spend?"

"As little as possible." He sounded cheap, but he had to be honest.

Cindy Mae's grand master expression fell. "How much is that?"

Ethan gestured to the ring. "Cindy Mae, I wouldn't pay a hundred dollars for the ring.

She huffed. "Amateurs." She waved the ring under his nose. "This is real platinum, Ethan, with real diamonds and real emeralds."

Grandpa laughed and motioned toward Cindy Mae. "This is why he brought me along. Shine it up."

೩

Julie waited at Peri's Perk for Grandma. Late afternoon, the coffee and sandwich café was quiet. Peri and her employees sat together at a table in the back, talking and drinking coffee.

Sipping her latte, Julie reviewed the yellow legal paper in front of her.

> *New dress*
> *Get nails and hair done.*
> *Cake by Ramona (if she has time)*
> *New shoes (definitely)*
> *Fresh flowers*
> *Invitations*
> *Buffet food (Grandma and Mom)*
> *Mom's linen, silver/china*

A few minutes later, Grandma came through the door, her cheeks a rosy red, her eyes sparkling. "Sorry I'm late."

Peri approached their table. "Hello, Mrs. Lambert. Can I get you anything?"

Grandma patted Peri's hand. "Yes, Matt raves about your chocolate toffee coffee. Let me try one of those."

Peri nodded. "Hot or cold?"

"Hot, please. There's a chill in the air today."

Julie moaned. "The weatherman says we're warming up starting tomorrow."

"Let's hope," Peri said. "Can I refresh your cup, Julie? On the house."

"Yes, thank you."

Peri hurried away. Julie slid her list across the table. "Can you think of anything else?"

Grandma perched her reading glasses on her nose and read. "Well, this is lovely, but I had a different thought in mind." She smiled widely.

Julie pulled the paper back across the table, an excitement stirring in her. "What?"

"Well, your first wedding was a big to-do. How about something simple but romantic and cozy this time."

Julie chewed on her bottom lip. *Hmm. . .* "Like what?"

"We could decorate our back deck and yard with white lights and build a big bonfire."

"Oh, we could wear jeans and sweaters."

"Matt could grill out. I could serve hot cider."

"Perfect, Grandma. I love it."

"Shall you enlist the Merewether Quartet?"

Scribbling on the paper, Julie agreed. "Yes, outdoor music. Kit can find someone to take my place, or just have the violins and viola play."

"We can hold the ceremony at twilight. I have plenty of white lights and candles from Christmas."

"Oh, candles." Julie added candles to the list. "I wanted a candlelight ceremony the first time, but Ethan said he would go crazy waiting until evening."

Grandma laughed. "He was ready to get married."

Julie leaned toward Grandma. "We loved each other, Grandma, but this ceremony is about a deeper commitment; it's about enduring love."

Grandma pressed her hand on Julie's. "I'm proud of you kids. You've endured difficulty and came out shining on the other side. I know many couples wouldn't have weathered such storms."

Julie tapped the corners of her eyes with her fingertips. "Only by God's grace." She blew her nose, then fired the do-or-die question at Grandma. "So how do we pull this off?"

Grandma flashed a sly smile. "I'm glad you asked. We haven't had a family gathering at our house since Christmas. I'll tell him we're having one of our barbecues. He can help your grandpa dig the fire pit."

She burst out laughing. "Then show up later for his own wedding."

"What a grand surprise."

Peri came with their coffee specialties as they discussed the ceremony details, divvying up the to-do list.

"When shall we do this?" Grandma asked as she jotted notes in her notepad.

Julie tapped the calendar on her electronic planner. "Let me phone Mom and see what their plans are for the next few weeks."

"Remember, your dad, Bobby, and Will leave for Costa Rica on a Sunday, mid-April, I think."

"Right. We could have the ceremony the Saturday before they go."

Grandma waved her hand at Julie. "Perfect."

Autodialing her parents' home phone, Julie mentioned to Grandma, "I can't spend a lot of money. Eth would kill me, but I do want this to be a surprise."

"Don't worry. I'm queen of the shoestring budget."

"Mom, hi, it's Julie." In one breath, she detailed the wedding plans with her mother.

"What a marvelous idea."

"How about a week from Saturday?" Julie chewed on her bottom lip and glanced out the window. *Oh no, Ethan and Grandpa.*

"No," her mom said. "Not the night before your father leaves for his golf trip. You know him."

Julie chewed her lower lip. "Yeah, right. I forgot about his travel neurosis."

Her mom laughed. "Yes, he'll want to pack, worry if he got everything, then pack some more and go to bed early. Why not have the ceremony Saturday?"

That's six days away. Julie looked at Grandma. "Think we can pull it off this Saturday?"

"Certainly." She sat up straight, ready for the challenge.

"This Saturday it is, Mom. I'll talk to you later. I've got to go; Ethan is coming."

"What?" Grandma glanced over her shoulder just as Ethan and Grandpa pushed through Peri's front door.

twenty-two

"What are you two doing here?" Ethan slipped his arm around Julie and kissed her forehead. He fought the sense of guilt over spending the money on the ring without telling her. He'd better give it to her soon or bust.

"Chatting." Julie smiled up at him, but he caught her tucking a yellow piece of paper into her satchel.

"Chatting?" He shifted his gaze to Grandma. She never could mask her feelings well. They were up to something.

"What are you boys up to, hmm?" Grandma asked.

"Yes," Julie echoed. "Why aren't you at work, Ethan?"

He grabbed her hand and held on. "Running errands."

"Yes, running errands," Grandpa parroted. "Lambert's Furniture stuff." He pulled up a stool and waved at Peri.

"Be right there, Mr. Lambert. The usual?"

"Yes, the usual."

"What about you, Ethan?" Peri called.

"Bring me what Julie's having." He sat next to Julie.

Covertly, he glanced at her hand and the small engagement ring he'd slipped on her ring finger a decade ago. He'd promised her a new one, but they could never afford it; then life got in the way. But today he changed all that.

Cindy Mae had polished the ring like Grandpa asked and showed it to Ethan. He'd never seen anything more beautiful. If a piece of jewelry could embody his wife, that piece did.

Cindy Mae wanted three thousand for it. Ethan shook his head, deflated. "Can't go that high."

Grandpa pulled out his wallet. "You put up what you got, Ethan. I'll cover the rest."

"Oh no, Grandpa, I can't let you do that. No." But his protest fell on deaf ears.

"I'll deduct it from your inheritance."

"What? Lambert's Furniture is my inheritance. I can't let you buy my wife a new ring."

"Then consider it a loan, interest free. You pay me back when you can, ten dollars at a time for all I care."

Just what I need, more debt. But he wanted the ring. "I don't know—"

Cindy Mae sighed and gazed toward the ceiling. "You two kill me. All right, twenty-five hundred."

So the deal was made. Cindy Mae agreed to redo the ring's shank and size it for free. Ethan could pick it up Friday. He couldn't wait to give it to her.

The sooner he gave Julie the ring, the better. He didn't think he could hide this expenditure too long. *Boy, it's hot in Peri's today. Am I sweating?*

"Here you go." Peri set a steaming, frothy coffee in front of him.

He handed it back to her. "Make it an ice coffee, please."

Julie regarded him. "Are you all right?"

He inhaled. "Sure. I'm fine."

"You're sweating." She pressed her hand on his forehead.

"I'm fine. Listen, how about dinner at the Italian Hills Saturday night? You and me?" The idea popped out of his mouth before his brain had time to meter his words. But he liked what he heard.

"Oh no, Ethan, we can't."

"Why not?"

"We're having a spring family barbecue." Grandma jumped into the discussion. "You'll need to help Grandpa dig the fire pit, get set up."

"When did this happen?" Grandpa asked.

"Just now, Matt." Grandma's firm tone surprised Ethan.

He faced Julie. "Then we can go on Friday."

"Um, no, I have quartet rehearsal. Let's go next week."

Ethan shrugged off his disappointment. He wanted to surprise Julie with the ring, but he didn't want to force it.

Lord, I'll submit to Your timing.

"It's okay; next week is fine."

❧

On her way home, Julie stopped by Bella's Cards & Gifts to pick up invitations. She and Grandma planned to hand deliver most of them, knowing some friends wouldn't be able to attend on such short notice, but this ceremony was not about a plethora of people or a mountain of gifts. It was about her and Ethan's renewed commitment.

She sat in bed pretending to read, filling out invitations instead. *I hope no one slips up in front of Ethan.*

Grandma called to say Ramona would make the cake, and she'd already enlisted several ladies from the women's Bible study to help make food.

"I told them to plan for fifty to sixty people. What do you think?" Grandma asked.

"That's a good estimate," Julie confirmed. "Thank you so much, Grandma."

Her mom had also called, excited. She'd found Great-Grandma's linens and discovered a Sinclair's sales ad for tea lights while throwing away the newspaper. She would pick some up tomorrow.

"And guess what! Your father said the weather would be sunny and warm this weekend."

"Mom, I appreciate your help."

"Oh, this is marvelous. . . ."

Snuggled now in her bed, writing invitations, Julie felt content. "What a great day, God. Thank You so much for all Your blessings."

Ethan's dark, wavy head popped around the bedroom door. "What are you doing?"

Julie tucked the invitations between the back pages of her book. "Reading."

Flopping on the bed, he took the book from her hand and drew her to him. "I need to tell you something."

She brushed her hand over his hair, her emotions vibrating

with a melody for her husband. "You seemed like something was bothering you tonight at Elizabeth and Kavan's."

"I spent some money, Julie."

She pushed herself upright. *Oh no, not again.* "On what?"

"You."

"Me?"

"I wanted to surprise you, but after my big money speech to you and hiding the Costa Rica trip, it didn't feel right."

Julie glanced around the room before looking Ethan in the eye. "What have you done with my husband? You look like him—"

"Come on, Jules. Help a guy out here."

She smoothed her hand over his chest and felt his heart beating. She knew it beat for her. "Do what you think is best. But don't spend too much money on me."

"Well, I won't buy a high-performance sports car, if that's what you mean."

She pinched his cheek. "Har, har. You love that car."

"I love you, Julie."

"I know you do. So what'd you buy me?"

He rolled off the bed and held up his hands. "It has to do with our conversation on the bridge the other night. That's all I'm saying."

"Really?" Her heart lurched, and she scrambled over to him. What did he do? Would it mess up her surprise? "Ethan, I need to tell you something."

He pulled off his sweater and disappeared into the closet. "Shoot."

"I spent some money, too. Well, I made plans to spend money."

He popped out of the closet. "On what?"

"On you."

"Me?"

"Well, not just you. You and me."

"How much?" He held his pajama bottoms in his hands.

"I don't know yet." She chewed her thumbnail.

"Less than a thousand?"

Julie gaped at him. "Did you spend a thousand dollars?"

"Did you?"

"No, I haven't spent anything yet, but I'll probably spend a couple hundred. I can keep it simple." Mentally, she ran down her checklist. She could pull off the ceremony without spending much, especially since she didn't need a fancy new dress or accessories. After all, it was a barbecue.

"What are you up to? Is that why you were with Grandma at Peri's? And what was on the yellow legal paper?"

She held up her hands. "Enough already. I'm not saying any more."

He grabbed her waist and tackled her to the bed.

"*Ack!* Ethan—" Her laugh filled the room.

"What are you up to, Mrs. Lambert?"

"Same as you, Mr. Lambert."

❧

On Saturday night, Ethan showered after helping Grandpa dig a bonfire and barbecue pit. He splashed on cologne and dressed in jeans and a white oxford shirt. He looked for his favorite navy sweater. It was missing, again.

Julie. . . He grinned and found a burgundy pullover to wear.

Julie had left hours ago to help Grandma set up, or so she said. Did she mention the quartet might play, too? With her hair rolled in large curlers, she'd dashed out the door. Then dashed back in.

"Oh, Will's going to pick you up tonight."

"What? Why? I can drive my car."

She shrugged. "So we can ride home together."

Jogging down the stairs, Ethan chuckled, thinking of his wife with her big curlers wanting to ride home with him after the barbecue. Giving up the Costa Rica trip and going to her in Florida were the best decisions he'd ever made besides marrying Julie.

Deep down, he suspected tonight had to do with Julie's surprise for him, but he felt clueless as to what, or how.

The doorbell rang. "Come in."

Will opened the door. "Are you ready to go?"

"Yes." Ethan stood in the kitchen, holding the pantry door open. *We still need to clean this out.* "Have you eaten yet?"

"Are you kidding? I'm waiting for Grandma's barbecue."

Ethan regarded his cousin. "Do you know what tonight is about?"

"Family gathering. Nothing out of the ordinary."

"So you say." Ethan slapped him on the back. "Let's swing by the diner. Get a little preparty dessert."

"I like your thinking."

They started out the door.

"Got your keys?" Will asked.

Ethan patted his pockets. "Check. Keys and wallet."

"Oh, hey—" Will pulled up short. "Grandpa said I should see that ring you bought Julie."

Ethan stopped on the porch step. "Now? You want to see it now?"

Will tipped his head and motioned over his shoulder with his thumb. "We're here, aren't we?"

Ethan furrowed his brow, shrugged, and ran upstairs to the bedroom with Will following. He'd hidden the ring in his sports bag, figuring Julie would never look there—for anything.

Will took the small red velvet box from him and lifted the top. He whistled low. "This set you back a bit. Do you need a raise?"

"No." Ethan reached for the box. Should he tell him about Grandpa's help?

Will examined the ring in the fading light of the window. "I'm definitely going to Cindy Mae if I ever need an engagement ring."

"She's got some beautiful stuff. Let's get going, or we won't have time for pie."

The phone rang as Ethan reached again for the ring box.

"You answer the phone; I'll put the ring away." Will stepped into the closet.

"Hello?"

It was Grandpa. "What are you doing? I need some help here."

Ethan chuckled. "Okay, we're on our way." He turned to Will. "Grandpa beckons."

"Let's go." Will patted him on the back and started downstairs.

"Did you put it in the pocket of the bag? I don't want to lose it."

"Yes, I put it in the pocket. The ring is safe. Let's go, or we won't have time to stop for preparty dessert."

"I'm with you, Cousin. I'm with you." Ethan followed Will downstairs and out the front door.

twenty-three

In Grandpa and Grandma's master bedroom, Julie slipped into a new pair of jeans and a blouse her mother had bought in Manchester.

"I couldn't resist." Her mother stood off to the side, hands folded together. "A woman has to have something new for her wedding. . .well, renewal ceremony."

Julie smiled at her. "Thank you, Mom. I love the clothes." She pulled on Ethan's navy merino wool sweater. "There, now I have something old, borrowed, and blue to go with the new."

Mom cried. Sniffling, she said, "I'll go check on how the ladies are progressing with the food." As she exited, Elizabeth came in.

"I've got red lipstick. But it's really red." She held up the wand for Julie to see.

She wrinkled her nose. "Not me."

"Didn't think so." Elizabeth closed that tube and opened another one. "This one is called blush. And it has sparklies in it."

Julie took the lipstick and striped it across her wrist. "Perfect."

Elizabeth raised her hands. "We have a winner. I'll take the red one down to Elle."

Julie made a face. "Elle? Bright red lipstick?"

"Yes, it's always the quiet ones, you know."

Julie laughed. "You're too funny, Beth." She watched her cousin-in-law exit, her middle slightly round with new life. Julie resolved to be the best "auntie" ever to the little Donovan.

Grandma bustled in after Elizabeth. "Oh, land sakes, I'm more nervous than at your first wedding. A barbecue wedding. What were we thinking?"

With a nervous giggle, Julie admitted, "It's going to be great.

The surprise element alone will be worth it."

"Your hair. It's still in curlers," Grandma said.

"I know. Michele hasn't made it here yet."

Just then, a tall redhead stumbled into the room, breathless. "Sorry I'm late."

"Well, speaking of—" Grandma said as Michele's bag of beauty tricks toppled to the floor.

Elizabeth came in right after Michele, followed by Mom again. As Michele and Elizabeth retrieved the contents of her bag, Elle entered.

"He's here."

Julie jumped. "He is?"

Elle nodded, her eyes wide with excitement.

"Oh no. Is Pastor Marlow here?" Julie jittered about, biting her bottom lip, while Michele took the curlers out of her hair.

"No, he's not."

Julie held up her hands. "Great. Don't let Ethan see him. He'll figure it out."

"I'm on it," Elle said.

"Oh, Elle." Julie darted after her.

"Julie!" Michele ripped the last roller out of the bride's head. "Stand still."

At the door, Julie reminded Elle, "Don't let the quartet play until I come out to the deck. That'll tip him off, too."

"Right."

"Have Grandpa or Dad put on a CD or something. The CD player is on the deck."

"Right again."

Elle went off on her mission, and Julie faced everyone in the room. "Am I a basket case? Yes, I'm a basket case."

All the voices rose to console her. Well, she had a right to be nervous. She was a bride after all. Even for a second time, it must go well. Especially the surprise part.

Michele jerked on her arm. "Sit down, or you're going down those stairs with a rat's nest for hair."

Julie sat in the chair and tried to relax. When she let herself exhale, she realized how fun it had been to plan the ceremony. She hoped Ethan liked his surprise.

What if he doesn't? She'd never considered that. She jumped to her feet and swerved around.

"Ow!" Michele dropped the hot flat iron to the floor.

"What if Ethan doesn't like his surprise?" She whipped around to Michele. "Sorry."

"Ethan will love his surprise," Mom reassured her.

Elizabeth added, "Didn't he ask you to marry him again?"

Julie fanned her face. "Okay, okay." She took a cleansing breath and sat down.

"Don't get up again." Michele had came at her with the flat iron, her lips pressed into a narrow line.

In fifteen minutes, Michele worked her magic, and everyone agreed Julie looked radiant and beautiful. "I even like the jeans," Grandma said.

As if on cue, her father tapped on the door. "It's time, Julie. We've maneuvered Ethan to the center of the deck, away from the bonfire smoke." He smiled. "But I'm not sure he'll stay there. He's asking for you."

"Thanks, Dad. I'm ready." Julie's gaze lingered on his angular face for a moment, thinking how much she loved him. He and Mom had taken the baby news as well as expected. Mom cried, and Dad cleared his throat, even disappeared for five minutes without warning. Yet they offered their love and support for whatever decisions she and Ethan would make concerning future children.

"Okay, Julie?" Dad's gentle voice interrupted her thoughts.

She cleared her head with a slight shake. "I'm sorry. I missed what you were saying."

He grinned. "Go down the front stairs and out the front door. Wait at the edge of the house until you hear the quartet play "Pachelbel's Canon." Then walk toward the deck steps. We'll all be waiting for you."

❧

Ethan leaned against the deck railing, arms folded over his

chest. "Where's Julie?" he asked Grandpa. "I see Kit and the quartet setting up, but no Julie."

Grandpa glanced around with a shrug. "She's coming."

Ethan shook his head. *Something's not right here. Is that Mrs. Hayes from Grandma's Bible study?* Mark Benton passed by with Sophia. This was not a typical Lambert gathering. *Something's definitely up.*

From the opposite end of Grandpa and Grandma's wide deck, Ethan heard the quartet begin to play. The family started gathering around. They all smiled at him. *What?*

"Ethan, over here." Will motioned for him to come by the steps.

"What's going on?" he asked in Will's ear.

"Look." Will nudged him.

Julie emerged from the shadows wearing his navy sweater, a small bouquet of flowers in her hand. His heart flip-flopped. Every sound, every person faded away in the light of her beauty.

She stopped at the top of the steps. "Hi, Ethan."

He tried to speak but couldn't. Suddenly Pastor Marlow stood beside him. "Here's your surprise, Ethan."

Low chuckles rippled through the crowd.

Julie grabbed his hand. "You asked me to marry you again. So we're getting married, *again.*"

His smile burst wide, and he rubbed his forehead. "How'd you. . . ? I mean—I had no idea. All of you knew?"

"Surprise!"

Pastor Marlow settled the intimate gathering. "Let's get these two married before they change their minds."

The friends and family laughed.

Pastor Marlow prayed, then instructed Ethan, "Face your bride, please."

"Gladly." Ethan turned to Julie, his *bride* for all time. He winked. "Nice sweater."

"I think so."

Marlow started, "Do you covenant with God to love this

woman as your wife, in laughter and sorrow, in disappointment and success, in poverty and riches, always remembering Lambert's Code?"

Ethan peered sideways at the pastor. The man was grinning. Shifting his gaze forward to Julie, he answered strong and sure, "Absolutely."

Pastor Marlow looked at Julie. "Do you covenant with God to love this man as your husband, in laughter and sorrow, in disappointment and success, in poverty and riches, always remembering Lambert's Code?"

Softly she said, "With my whole heart."

"Then I declare you husband and wife for a second time. Let no one separate what God has joined together."

While everyone cheered, Ethan snatched her into his arms and twirled her around. When he set her down, he heard Pastor Marlow ask for the ring.

Julie leaned toward him and said in a low voice, "There is no ring, Pastor."

Ethan winced. He had a ring—a perfect ring for a perfect occasion. But it wasn't here. It was at home, safe and sound in his smelly sports bag.

"How about this ring?" Will stepped forward and handed the pastor the red velvet box.

"I thought you put it back in the pocket." Ethan's eyes followed his cousin as he returned to his spot among the family.

"I did. My pocket." He tapped his jacket pocket and winked.

Ethan shook his head, grinning. *A conspiracy.*

Julie gasped when Ethan slipped the ring on her finger. "Ethan, it's beautiful. Oh my, I don't know what to say." Her hand trembled in his.

"Repeat after me," Pastor Marlow instructed. "Let this ring be a sign and seal of our covenant and pledge."

Ethan repeated the words with vigor. Then he added a vow of his own. "Babe, you are number one in my life: before sports, before work, before everything."

Her green eyes sparkled.

Pastor Marlow turned to Julie. "You don't have a ring, but repeat after me."

"Okay." Her gaze never shifted from Ethan's. He thought his heart might explode. Every ounce of heartache that led to this moment almost seemed worth it. Almost.

"Let this ring be a sign and seal of our covenant and pledge."

Softly Julie made her promise. Like Ethan, she added a few words of her own. "I promise to respect you by never keeping bad news from you and by consulting you on future car purchases." She squeezed his hand. "I love you, Ethan."

"I love you, Julie." He drew her to him.

"Ethan," Pastor Marlow said, "you may kiss your bride."

So he did.

epilogue

Six months later

Julie cradled little Matthew Lambert Donovan in her arms, breathing in the scent of his newborn skin. With her fingers, she smoothed his soft, dark curls.

"He's beautiful, Elizabeth."

"I'm still amazed. He's a week old, and I can't imagine life without him."

Ethan marched into the nursery. "Where's my new cousin?" He sounded like a general looking for his troops.

"Shh, Ethan, he's right here." Julie settled Baby Matt in his arms.

Ethan stared down at him. His voice was husky when he said, "He's so little."

Kavan wrapped his arm around Elizabeth. "Listen, you two, please don't feel obligated, but we'd like you to be Matt's guardians. You know, in case something happens to Elizabeth and me."

Julie waved off the comment. "Come on, nothing's going to happen to you two. Please."

"Well, we hope not, but just in case, we'd want Matt to be raised by you guys."

Julie peered at Ethan. By reading his expression, she knew the answer without asking.

Elizabeth added, "Please, think and pray about it. We understand if you don't—"

"We'd love to," Ethan blurted, then gave Julie a sheepish grin. "If you agree."

"Of course I agree." She kissed Baby Matt tenderly.

Kavan smiled at Elizabeth. "Wonderful."

Later in the evening, sitting around the dining room table slicing pieces of chocolate cake, Kavan asked, "Have you two decided yet?"

Julie cut a piece of cake. "We're getting there."

Ethan picked up an empty plate when Elizabeth shoved the cake his way. "I've investigated several adoption agencies." He cut a large piece of cake.

"But we won't do anything until we get back from Paris with Kit in the spring," Julie said.

Ethan took a bite of cake, snickering. "Kit's at our apartment more than her own home. She said since she doesn't have children, she adopted us."

Julie sighed, feeling content and peaceful. While she and Ethan looked into having children, they'd found a *mom*. Instead of adopting, they were adopted.

Right now, Kit needed them as much as any woman needed a child. Only the Lord could have orchestrated such a union.

Elizabeth sat back, cake plate in her hands. "I'll be adopted for a trip to Paris."

They laughed and talked about Kit, babies, and adoption, and Elizabeth poured glasses of milk. "Let's eat all the cake," she said.

"Here, here!"

This is true family. This is right, Julie thought. In her heart, she thanked the Lord for His grace and for teaching her and Ethan the beauty of submitting to one another.

Callie's MOUNTAIN

3 stories in 1

More than one story is needed to share Callie Duncan's journey to climb the mountain of past experiences to see out over a valley full of future possibilities. Will what she learns about love pull her through the challenges of life and allow her to teach others? Titles by author Veda Boyd Jones.

Contemporary, paperback, 352 pages, 5³⁄₁₆" x 8"

A Letter To Our Readers

Dear Reader:

In order that we might better contribute to your reading enjoyment, we would appreciate your taking a few minutes to respond to the following questions. We welcome your comments and read each form and letter we receive. When completed, please return to the following:

Fiction Editor
Heartsong Presents
PO Box 719
Uhrichsville, Ohio 44683

1. Did you enjoy reading *Lambert's Code* by Rachel Hauck?
   ❏ Very much! I would like to see more books by this author!
   ❏ Moderately. I would have enjoyed it more if

   _____

   _____

   _____

2. Are you a member of **Heartsong Presents**? ❏ Yes ❏ No
   If no, where did you purchase this book? _____

   _____

3. How would you rate, on a scale from 1 (poor) to 5 (superior), the cover design? _____

4. On a scale from 1 (poor) to 10 (superior), please rate the following elements.

   ____ Heroine   ____ Plot
   ____ Hero   ____ Inspirational theme
   ____ Setting   ____ Secondary characters

5. These characters were special because? _____
_____
_____

6. How has this book inspired your life? _____
_____
_____

7. What settings would you like to see covered in future
   Heartsong Presents books? _____
_____
_____

8. What are some inspirational themes you would like to see
   treated in future books? _____
_____
_____

9. Would you be interested in reading other **Heartsong
   Presents** titles? ❑ Yes ❑ No

10. Please check your age range:
    ❑ Under 18   ❑ 18-24
    ❑ 25-34   ❑ 35-45
    ❑ 46-55   ❑ Over 55

Name _____
Occupation _____
Address _____
City, State, Zip_____